T0275083

LOWEST COMMON DENOMINATOR

LOWEST COMMON DENOMINATOR

PIRKKO SAISIO

TRANSLATED FROM FINNISH BY
MIA SPANGENBERG

TWO LINES
PRESS

Originally published as *Pienin yhteinen jaettava*
Copyright © 1998 by Pirkko Saisio
Published originally in Finnish by WSOY
Published in agreement with Helsinki Literary Agency and Regal
Hoffmann and Associates
Translation copyright © 2024 by Mia Spangenberg

Two Lines Press
582 Market Street, Suite 700, San Francisco, CA 94104
www.twolinespress.com

ISBN: 978-1-949641-71-4
Ebook ISBN: 978-1-949641-72-1

Cover Design by Rafael Nobre
Typeset by Stephanie Nisbet

Library of Congress Cataloging-in-Publication Data
Names: Saisio, Pirkko, 1949- author. | Spangenberg, Mia M., translator.
Title: Lowest common denominator / Pirkko Saisio ; translated from the
Finnish by Mia Spangenberg.
Other titles: Pienin yhteinen jaettava. English
Description: San Francisco, CA : Two Lines Press, 2024.
Identifiers: LCCN 2024005190 (print) | LCCN 2024005191 (ebook) |
ISBN 9781949641714 (hardcover) | ISBN 9781949641721 (ebook)
Subjects: LCGFT: Bildungsromans. | Queer fiction. | Novels.
Classification: LCC PH355.S2146 P5413 2024 (print) | LCC PH355.
S2146 (ebook) | DDC 894/.54133--dc23/eng/20240222
LC record available at https://lccn.loc.gov/2024005190
LC ebook record available at https://lccn.loc.gov/2024005191

1 3 5 7 9 10 8 6 4 2

This work has been published with the financial support of
FILI – Finnish Literature Exchange and is supported in part by an award
from the National Endowment for the Arts.

she

The first time it happened I was eight years old.

It was a November morning.
The street was black and shiny, swollen behind the windows wet with sleet.
I saw myself in the window: a chubby, bad-tempered child.
I pulled on wool socks too tight for my feet.
A button was missing from my vest. Mother took a five-mark bill out of her purse.
I stuffed it in my sock.

And that's when it happened.

I wrote a sentence in my mind: *She didn't want to wake up.*
I changed the sentence: *She didn't want to get up yet.*
I added another sentence to the first: *She was too tired to go to school.*
And then I improved the second sentence: *She was just too, too tired to go to school.*

I looked triumphantly at Father, who was in his shirt-sleeves drinking black coffee and reading the *Työkansan Sanomat* newspaper.

Mother stood by the entryway mirror spreading a touch of rouge from her lips to her cheeks as she hummed "Harbor Nights."

Neither of them noticed that I had become *she*, the one always under observation.

The heat hadn't let up, even though it was already September. I'd been gone for two weeks.

The linden trees on Pohjoisranta street dangled their dusty leaves, tired and dispirited. Even the new windows were sticky and covered in dust. The apartment was overflowing with stiff plastic sheeting. The chairs, books, Tibetan thangkas, and a painting of an African orchestra she'd bought in Stockholm shone from underneath the plastic ice like remnants from the *Titanic*.

The windows had been replaced while I was in Korea.

I removed the souvenirs from my suitcase. Lost in the sea of plastic, the Korean objects looked absurd, like tiny shipwrecks.

My fever rose; I'd already had it for over a week.

I smiled and said something, but not about the fever.

It was time to be a mother again, and a partner.

And a daughter.

In Korea I'd settled in the heart of old Seoul, which excavators, McDonald's restaurants, concrete office buildings, and parking garages were crowding into an ever-shrinking corner.

On the street, in front of the hotel, the cables had been pulled out of the ground, so you could only enter the hotel by crossing over a series of planks thrown across the fistula cut into the earth.

But the old Korea emerged behind the black lacquered door.

In the center of the courtyard grew a tree. Though bent, it thrust its branches tirelessly toward the sun.

A clay oven stood next to the tree. Empty Coca-Cola crates were stacked in front of the firebox. The clay oven was no longer in use, as the hotel was scheduled for demolition.

Sliding paper doors enclosed the courtyard. Each opened into a room about thirty square feet in size where, at night, a thin bast mat was spread on the dirt floor.

Before the building became a hotel, these rooms had been home to an extended family including grandparents and parents, children and in-laws.

The grandparents had been in charge then, and everyone would gather to eat rice and kimchi in the courtyard, by the oven.

The oven had released its smoke through a narrow flue. Now dust clouds, kicked up by the excavators, circled high in the sky.

The elderly innkeepers, always smiling, pretended not to notice the clouds.

We hotel guests in search of the past coughed into our handkerchiefs.

The number of planks we had to cross to reach the hotel grew with each passing day.
Soon we could only come and go via the back door.
It opened into an alley that smelled of urine and fish guts.
As I carried my suitcase to the taxi—the driver had refused to drive up to the hotel—I saw a German tourist dressed in hiking clothes carefully remove a ceramic decoration from one of the hotel's eaves with a Swiss army knife.

I didn't place a call to Hämeentie road until evening.
I had to wait a long time for the phone to be answered.
Father's voice was tired and depressed, again.
"It's just me calling."

Her voice was soft, honeyed somehow.
She had started talking to her father as if he were a child.

"Oh. All right then."
Then Father put the receiver on the table.
I took a sip of Calvados. I'd bought it in Paris on my way back home. It tasted faintly of smoke and even more faintly of apples. Aged twenty-four years, it was

just what a good Calvados was supposed to taste like, but I still couldn't enjoy it. My fever sent nasty shivers up my legs and spine.

A minute passed, then another.

I heard rustling, the clatter of a cane, the familiar cough. Then:

"All right. I got a chair. So you're home."

"Yeah. I got back just an hour ago."

Why did she lie?

"All right. I see."

"Yeah."

I sipped more Calvados. It burned my throat, and my brow broke into a sweat, then just as quickly cooled.

"You sure do travel. All the time."

"It was a business trip."

She was on the defensive.

For some reason she felt the need to defend herself.

"So how are you?" I asked.

"Can't complain."

"Hmm."

"Just hanging on. This life."

"That's how it is. In the end."

She swayed to the rhythm of her father's voice like an aquatic plant in the warm currents of the ocean.

"Sure does."
"Yeah."
"That's life."
"Right."
"Yeah."
"How's Kerttu?"

Kerttu was eighty-six. Father called Kerttu his girlfriend. When she had first met Kerttu ten years ago, Kerttu sat in the same armchair once occupied by Mother, and then after Mother's death by other women who had since disappeared including Aune, Lempi (who drank vermouth and played solitaire at eight in the morning), and Siviä (whom Father had found through an ad for a pen pal). Kerttu had been a stylish, elderly widow, the type who coughed daintily as she sipped the cognac she'd been offered with coffee. In the ten years Father had known her, he'd introduced her to whiskey, Koskenkorva and Smirnoff Vodka, sweet berry liqueurs, beer, and gin long drinks.

"They take her away every evening."
"Kerttu?"
"Yeah."
"Where to?"
"I don't know."

Father's voice has grown agitated.
She's forced to give up her pleasant, feverish swaying.

"So where do they take her?"

"Well, wherever they take old people. They don't tell me anything."

I light a cigarette. It tastes like fever.

"Who takes her?"

"Raimo. Her son. He picks her up and takes her away every night in his car. Every night, I'm telling you."

"Oh dear."

"Yeah."

More rustling on the line.

Now the rustling is impatient.

"Maybe you could call," I hear Father's timid voice.

"Who?"

"Those people."

A pause. It stretches unbearably.

I need to take my temperature, she thinks.

"All right, I'll call," I lie.

"Yes, do."

"Yep."

"They'll tell you."

I don't have the energy for this.

To be a daughter. Today. When I have a fever.

Why am I thinking of myself as her *again?* she wonders.

"I'll stop by tomorrow," I say, lowering my voice so it's even softer.

"You do that."

"I'd come today, but it seems I have a bit of a fever."
"Oh."
"Hang in there."
"Got to."
"See you tomorrow."

She puts down the receiver and looks out the kitchen window into the courtyard.
The building superintendent is sweeping, wiping his brow as he works.
The flowers poking out of the wooden window boxes look burned in the evening sun.
This summer is never going to end.

That night I found myself transported to Fleminginkatu street again.
Mother had returned from a long trip, but she had no suitcase.
Cheerfully absent, Mother sat in her armchair, wearing her Bucharest Festival skirt with the people of the world dancing hand in hand along the hem.
I stood at the front door trying to think of a word or a sentence or a song that would stop Mother from leaving again.
A ray of sunshine pierced through the curtains, casting deep shadows under her eyes and along her sharp nose.
Mother smiled to herself. She didn't look at me.

Then I woke up. My fever had gone down slightly.

I called Father as early as nine.
No one answered.
At ten I called Raimo.
Raimo told me he'd taken Kerttu to a memory care home the previous Tuesday and hadn't been to see Father since.
I set off for Hämeentie road right away.
But

she stops as soon as she reaches Pohjoisranta street, because between the tired linden trees she glimpses a schooner with scarlet sails gliding serenely along the oil-smooth sea.
She commits the scene to memory.
She needs the schooner, the sea, and this moment, and she prays it would end here and now so she wouldn't have to go to Hämeentie, open the door, and find what she already knows is waiting for her.

The previous summer, in June, Father sold the cabin.
I didn't look at the lake when I went to collect my things, but I knew it must be glittering, just as I knew the birch trees must be celebrating the lushness of early summer the same way they'd been celebrating it for the past twenty-eight years.

In November, Father went to the health clinic to get a cane, and in January, he put the car up for sale.

As the Lada disappeared from view, Father grabbed my arm, then, noticing his mistake, supported himself on the garage's concrete wall instead.

"Got nothing left now."

In March we buried our relative Jopi.

I got Father a pastrami sandwich and caramel cake from the buffet table in the funeral home that had sprung up next to Malmi Cemetery; in recent years I'd learned the buffet offerings by heart.

"Everyone ends up going," Father said,

and

again she had to flee the rundown hopelessness in Father's voice, so amid the quietly burning, indifferent candles and the hostile clinking of coffee cups she found herself somewhere else, far away, on a shining, shoreless sea in her boat that smelled of gasoline, a boat that in her daydream wasn't rotten at all but a proud sailboat cutting rigidly through the waves on a journey far away. Somewhere far away.

In July we buried Sisko, my godmother.

Father waited for me in front of the chapel in a white tracksuit.

His tie was in his coat pocket. Father could no longer tie it himself, and Kerttu couldn't remember the steps for the complicated knot.

The laces on Father's sneakers were undone.
I bent down to tie them and led him into the chapel.
I got Father a pastrami sandwich and caramel cake from
the buffet table. I cut the sandwich into bite-sized pieces
and put a piece of cake on his spoon, which Father was
able to guide to his mouth.
And

she felt uneasy and guilty about the intense looks of
approval and pity momentarily trained on her: *Now
look, there's a good daughter.*

I rang Father's doorbell. (Twenty-nine years ago it had
been my doorbell, too.)
Silence on the other side.
I rang the doorbell again.
Then I peeked through the mail slot, but the inner door
was closed.
I lit a match to illuminate the threshold.
His newspapers lay there untouched.
The light went out in the stairwell.
And

she stands in the darkness, wishing she could fall into
the soundless ellipsis of time and find herself somewhere else, far away from this dark stairwell.
But instead

I switched on the light again and tried to focus.

I need to hurry, I tried thinking.

I rang the neighbor's doorbell—somehow I managed.

No one came to the door.

I rang the doorbells on Father's floor—somehow I managed to ring them all.

No one came to their doors, and then

she finds herself in the elevator.

After the elevator comes the front door and a long stretch of pavement.

She sees herself running down Hämeentie road, feverish and out of breath.

She sees herself wishing a police car would pull up, and a police officer would step out with a key and tell her what to do next.

She sees herself running to the police station to get an answer and a key and permission to enter her father's home, her home.

She's almost reached the station and the answer and the key when

two drunken men approached me, their arms around each other's shoulders.

Hämeentie rumbled indifferently, showing no concern for me, and I realized one of the men was an old childhood friend.

Afraid he would ask me about Father right then and there, I dove into a Chinese restaurant.

I crashed into booth after booth until I was stopped by a

menu thrust into my hands by a Chinese waiter.

"*Huva päivä,*" the waiter tried to greet me in his best Finnish.

And

she sees herself sitting on a soft bench in a booth, studying the menu.

This is ridiculous, she thinks.

I need to do something, she admonishes herself.

This is a nightmare—her next thought.

Or a scene from a Woody Allen movie.

I need to think straight, right now.

And

getting up from the booth and apologizing to the baffled waiter, I rush out the door into the street and I don't stop until I'm inside the subway station.

I buy a ticket; I don't remember where I'm going, but I do remember I have a fever, a very high fever.

I remember that Father is behind two locked doors and unable to retrieve his newspapers from the threshold, and yet

she stands by the ticket machine and lets the rumbling from the tunnel take her away from this time and place, somewhere far away.

A Romani woman's abundant skirts have gotten caught in the escalator, and with dazed satisfaction she hears the quick footsteps of the subway guards and the screeching of the escalator as it's forced to a halt; she watches as a steady, noisy stream of families, Japanese tourists, unhurried drunkards, retirees in white hats, veiled Muslim women, Somalis, Senegalese, and exasperated Finnish children flushed from the heat all rush past.

She has time to imagine she's back at the National Museum of Korea, in front of a display case in which a doll, galloping at full pelt, wears a golden helmet with wings on the sides, and she realizes the wings look just like flames before suddenly remembering where she is again.

I need to think straight runs through her mind, and she rips herself out of her sleepy delirium.

She only needs to walk from the ticket machine to the kiosk in the tunnel.

I need a pen—her next desperate thought—and she repeats it out loud to the salesperson at the kiosk.

The salesperson stares at her in surprise.

Did I say it wrong? she wonders, but now the salesperson is smiling.

"A pencil or a pen?"

I have to make a decision! she thinks in a panic.

"How about a pencil," she chooses randomly.

"I'm sorry, but we don't have any."

And the salesperson smiles again.

The salesperson is a soft, ample girl whose Savo accent is already receding.

And now

I wish I could stay right here and press my head into the valley formed by her soft, undulating breasts and complain about my fate, about how hard it is to be a mother and a partner and a daughter at this very moment.

But

she still has some fight left—she has to.

"A pen then."

"I'm sorry, we don't have pens either."

Now she sees herself standing helplessly in the shadow of the girl with her smile and her undulating breasts, but she won't let herself vanish from this time and place again.

"*Perkele*," she hears herself curse, calmly rolling the *r*. "Every kiosk sells pens."

And she fixes her eyes on a ballpoint pen lying unsuspectingly on a graph-ruled notebook.

"That's a pen right there," she hears herself say triumphantly.

"It belongs to the staff."

A menacing, cool draft of air ripples up from the depths of that warm Savo accent.

"I'm taking it," she hears herself say,

and

I'm forced to run back along Hämeentie, trying to remember why it was so important to get a pen.

At the door to the stairwell I remember: I need to call the building superintendent.

I need to go into the stairwell and find the super's phone number in the directory and go to a phone booth and call to get a key to the door so I can open it and find Father, dead or alive.

The super unlocks the door.
"All right," I say.
The bathroom door is open.
Father is on the floor in his underwear, grasping the washing machine's drain hose, nails white.
One of his cheeks is blue.
The super stands on the doormat in the entryway.
I stand at the bathroom door.
"Well then," says the super. "I guess you won't be needing me here."
"Guess not," I say, and before I go to Father, I fish a hundred-mark bill and the kiosk pen out of my pocket and sign the receipt for opening the door.
The super leaves. The door clicks shut,
and

time refuses to budge.
Now she's the one standing on the doormat, the one who doesn't know what to do.
Yawning, she remembers her fever.
She brushes her hand over the phone, and only then does she manage to step into the bathroom.
Her father's eyelids twitch.
"Hey," she says, not knowing where to put the pen she compulsively shifts from one hand to the other.
The pen feels sullied; it's been violated by her cold, sticky sweat.

Her father's lips move, and after a moment's hesitation, she puts her ear to his blue-tinged lips and toothless mouth.

"You came. After all."

green cap; yellow airplane

I'm an only child.

But I have so many people around me, it takes me a while to realize it.

There's Mother.
At first Mother is always home, but later she goes to work at Irja Markkanen's corner store and I end up in preschool.
Mother wears a white lace blouse, even on weekdays, and it has beige buttons.
At home, Mother usually listens to the radio or sings Russian battle songs; she was a member of the Finland–Soviet Union Society Performers when she was younger.
Sirpakka used to be in the same troupe, which is why Mother lets her in, even though Sirpakka is always drunk, which isn't appropriate for women.
Sirpakka is from Varkaus, just like Mother, but while Sirpakka has gone astray, Mother has not.
When Sirpakka brings Mother a bouquet, Mother unwraps it in the kitchenette and finds a bottle of

Koskenkorva Vodka inside, already opened.

Sirpakka drinks the rest while Mother sits on the bed, anxiously glancing at the clock and hoping Sirpakka leaves before Father comes home from work.

Father calls Sirpakka *Ronttonen*, or "Old Shoe."

Father has thick, curly hair and wears a wool cardigan with moose on it, knit by Grandma.

Father works for the Finland–Soviet Union Society.

On weekends he travels around the country showing Soviet films, teaching Finns about socialism's achievements and that sort of thing.

Aunt Ulla visits often.

Aunt Ulla has a gorgeous green coat made of soft, faux fur.

Her black velvet hat is studded with gold stars.

Aunt Ulla prefers to visit when Father isn't home.

Father and Aunt Ulla don't get along very well, because Aunt Ulla once voted for a candidate from the center-right National Coalition Party simply for his beautiful brown eyes.

Aunt Ulla is Mother's big sister.

We get plenty of visitors, and most don't mind if Father is home.

Lots of people come over for meetings.

But these people are boring; they take minutes at our only table, and I have to be quiet and play all by myself. I'm the only child at the meetings, but that's not what makes me an only child—it's far more serious and complicated.

When people Mother knows from her troupe visit, or when the sewing club meets, or when Father's relatives come to see us, there are plenty of other children around—but I'm still considered an only child.

Being an only child means, for instance, that the children out in the courtyard act jealous of my Sunday walks with my parents, of my not having to get up at eight on Sunday mornings to go to Sunday school like they do, because Mother and Father and I don't believe in those things.

I get everything I want, and I don't have to share anything with anyone—that's what everyone says—and so I'm at risk of growing up to be selfish and ambitious.

It may even be inevitable.

Everyone says Mother is young and beautiful, and I agree.

But then they go on to say Mother is young and beautiful because she's only bothered to have one child.

They say Father is handsome and a proper family man who doesn't appear interested in booze.

That makes me happy, but then they go on to say that, if push came to shove, they doubt Father could hold his own against a real man, one of those men who drinks and beats their wife and children on Saturdays after the sauna, because they've been to war and have shrapnel in their heads.

I ask at home about this war and shrapnel business, then

go back to the others and explain that Father served in the coastal artillery on the island of Suomenlinna and was never injured, thanks to Stalin and the fact that it was more important for the Soviet Union to win WWII than to conquer an insignificant country like Finland.

Someone says they hate to break it to me, but it was Finland that beat the Soviet Union and not the other way around, and besides, the coastal artillery was never involved anyway.

And so yet again I'm the only child whose father wasn't at the decisive Battle of Raate Road or even at one of the battles fought in the village of Summa.

Much later she finds out her father is also an only child. But first she has to swallow the shocking fact that her father was once a child.

It's far too overwhelming to believe that Grandma wasn't born a grandmother but was and still is a mother, her father's mother.

And that before becoming a grandmother and a mother, Grandma was also a child and someone's daughter.

At least Grandma looks like herself in her class picture from Kallio Elementary School, even though she's so small and young with a big nose and lace collar.

But the bald, chubby, sour-faced child posed on the sofa in knee-high boots can't possibly be her father, because her father is thin and lively with curly hair.

Grandma's album also has photographs of a little girl with a bow in her hair wearing something so flouncy it's impossible to tell if it's a skirt or a pair of pants.

And when Grandma tells her the child in the picture isn't a girl at all but her father, she gasps in astonishment. Because

I don't yet know that Grandma and Grandpa had a little girl before Father was born who died at the age of two, and that Father was forced to wear bows and dresses throughout his early childhood in her place. And it's only

much, much later that she learns her mother and father had a boy before she was born. He died when he was only four days old.

I would like to be a boy.
It's not a problem at first.
I can pee standing up, and do so when no one is watching, even though it's hard and messy and I splash a little.
My hair is cut short since it's so thin, and once I learn to whistle, swear, and spit, people often think I'm a boy, at least in summertime when I get to wear wide-legged pants.
I hate girls, and I don't know any either.
Alf, Reiska, and Risto are my best friends, and one of them always agrees to be the mother when we play house.
I'm the father. In the mornings I go to work showing Soviet films, and when I come home Reiska, Risto, or Alf has dinner ready on the table.

I'm going to be a father when I grow up.

Aunt Ulla admits she wanted to be a boy when she was little, too.
But Mother and Grandma torment me by twisting my thin hair into curlers and putting me in ruffled, floral-print dresses with starched aprons.
Father is taking a correspondence course to become a salesman and says he wants me to grow up to be a woman who can hold her own against any man, like a mining engineer or a woman with a doctorate in Economics and Business Administration, or a cool-headed businesswoman like Hella Wuolijoki, the leftist timber merchant; Father sometimes chauffeurs Wuolijoki in her BMW until he buys it for himself.

Grandpa says everyone should leave me alone.
If I want to be a boy, then I'm a boy: simple as that.

And Grandpa's the one who bought me the green cap, the one with the yellow plastic airplane on the crown—I'm sure of it.

I don't like getting new clothes.
Clothing stores frighten me.
Whenever I'm fitted for a new coat or snow bib, I start to cry.
"Good Lord," Father says, and Mother:
"Now let's not get all worked up."

Eventually I'm no longer taken to clothing stores. I won't end up in one again for years.

I do still have to go to shoe stores, but they don't frighten me the way clothing stores, hair salons, and photography studios do. And preschool.

In shoe stores your feet are put inside an X-ray machine that measures whether your feet will fit the shoes you want to buy.

You can see the bones in your feet on the X-ray machine.

Soon clothes start appearing in our home.

After the Pollaris visit, for example, they leave flowers, sweaters, and aprons behind, alongside dirty coffee cups and the plates we'd used to serve marble cake.

I know the aprons and sweaters are clothes my second cousin Helena has outgrown, and that Aunt Kaarina, Helena's mother, has supposedly left them here by accident.

But no one knows that Helena is the only person in the whole world whose apron I'm willing to wear.

Helena's apron smells freshly ironed and of detergent, but no one knows I can detect another smell underneath: Helena's own smell.

Helena has the curliest hair and is the most beautiful person I know.

And the smartest person I know.

Helena knows how to draw and has dimples and a good sense of humor, too.

Grandpa used to like Helena more than any other little girl in the world, so I'm told.

Before I was born, so they say.

I would like to be Helena.
But I know I never will be because I'm bad and dark-haired and don't have dimples.

But even Helena doesn't have a green cap.
I do.
One day it's there, on the dinner table, parked right between the liver sauce and the bread.
With a yellow airplane made of real plastic on the crown.
It's a boy's cap—there's no doubt about it.
And it's all mine, because it's too small for Father, and Mother wouldn't be caught dead in a boy's cap.
I've wanted one for a long time, as long as I've wanted lederhosen, a cap gun, a water gun, a bow and arrow, and a pedal car—all things I'll never get.
But the cap is mine.
For me alone.
I put the cap on my head and look at myself in the entryway mirror.

It's a mistake.

Because now something shifts within her.
She can tell by the way Mother doesn't say anything.
And neither does Father or Grandma. No one says a thing, not even Aunt Ulla.
She can tell her cap is in danger.

And so she guards it closely.

She puts it on first thing in the morning.

She wears it at the cutting board in the kitchenette, eating her oatmeal.

She wears it perched on the kitchenette's windowsill, dropping sausage skins out onto the street below until Mother tells her to go outside and play.

And when it's time for her nap, her cap is right next to her on her pillow, as she drowsily strokes its soft green surface and the sharp plastic edges of the yellow airplane.

But no matter how fiercely I guard my little green cap, it disappears one day.

I look for it on the hat rack, under the bed, and in the kitchenette's cabinets, but I can't find it anywhere.

No one helps me look for it, and I begin to have the sneaking suspicion that my cap is gone for good.

"That was a boy's cap," Mother tries to console me.

"Everybody would have laughed at you," Father says.

"The Big Bad Wolf took it, there's no point looking for it." That's Aunt Ulla.

She knows all about the Big Bad Wolf.

It's the very same wolf that took her pacifier and prompted her first memory.

I'm two years old, but I don't know that.

I'm sitting in an enamel washbasin filled with warm water.

A fire hums steadily in the stove; we're at Grandma's house.

Skirts and pants bustle around me, as does a big, furry creature called a dog or Tepsi.

The dog licks me as she walks past. Her breath smells bad.

She couldn't have known the word for dog, and she didn't know what a fire or a stove were either. But she could sense them.

This memory can't be wrong.

She melts into a blissful state in the warm, soapy water, surrounded by the blazing fire, the footsteps, the murmuring voices.

My mouth is full and tastes of old rubber. I've chewed my pacifier in half. It's blood-red, and warm drool runs down my chin, trickling over my bare tummy into the soapy water.

A hand appears. It approaches from above, like almost everything does.

The hand snatches the pacifier from my mouth.

The skirts and pants form a wall around me, and my pacifier is passed from one hand to the next amid all the skirt hems and pant legs.

"Binky!" I cry, extending my arm, but I'm given a strange, hard, blue pacifier instead.

A door under the kitchen counter is opened, and I watch my old pacifier hurtle into darkness.

I hear a splash from the slop bucket.

Then silence.

"The Big Bad Wolf got it," Grandma says.

The Big Bad Wolf covets things that are important to people, so important they can't live without them.
The Big Bad Wolf leaves an endless desert of desires and substitutes in his wake.

I never liked that hard, blue pacifier. It never grew warm in my mouth, and its sharp edges pressed against my nose. Mother and Father and Aunt Ulla and Grandma and Grandpa were all pleased with their childrearing method:
"We got that girl off her pacifier in one go!"
And

she did get over the pacifier, but not the cap.
Of course, the pacifier required its own string of endless substitutes: tough, sticky taffy; hard chewing gum; long, wet kisses; beer drunk straight from the bottle; and eventually, cigars and cigarettes, which were to become a painful and pleasurable addiction.
But there was nothing that could make up for her lost green cap.
It demanded to be replaced by other caps, and as soon as she earned her first paycheck, she rushed out to buy herself a stiff, uncomfortable, blue-and-black-striped cap like those worn by railroad workers.
She was pudgy and pimply—a typical teenager dissatisfied with life—and it wasn't until she saw a photo of herself that she realized the cap didn't suit her.

And still that uncomfortable cap was followed by soft, round Marimekko caps (one pink with light-green stripes, the other light blue with dark-blue stripes).

At university she wore big Kangol caps, and much later, caps with plastic brims advertising things like Kansa insurance, Karjala beer, and the Finnish Workers' Sports Federation tournaments.

After that were the Greek fisherman hats, which she collected by the dozen.

Then came the baseball hats (a bright yellow one advertising Radio Mafia and a dark-red one advertising Q-Theater).

And in between were hundreds of failed, impersonal hats that she donated to the Salvation Army or UFF secondhand stores and then forgot.

But

where is the green cap with the yellow plastic airplane on the crown?

And where is the little girl who stubbornly wore the green cap as she watched the Bolshoi Ballet on tour in Helsinki even though she'd been told that no one wears a hat during a performance?

And who calmly replied:

"Well I do."

dream writing

Her book would never be finished if she didn't retrieve the basil that had frozen and turned black.
The basil was in her cat Aleksei's stomach, because he had eaten it.
Aleksei slept at her feet.
She took a pair of scissors and cut the cat open.
She retrieved the basil.
Aleksei lay on the blanket, cut in two, still alive.
She turned hot and cold, then woke up.

Her heart hammered in her chest, and beads of sweat cooled on her forehead.
But her cat lay at her feet, squinting sleepily.
Relieved, she tried to go back to sleep.

She felt something cold against her leg.
Opening her eyes, she saw the frozen basil and the scissors encrusted with frost on the sheets.
She sat up to pet her cat.
He was cut down the middle, and both halves cried out in pain.

She woke up again.

Her heart hammered in her chest, and beads of sweat cooled on her forehead.
She groped for her cat in the dark. He was gone.

But she still couldn't work on her novel for over three weeks.
The frozen basil tormented her.
She was tormented by the price of writing.

I'm standing in the hallway of Maria Hospital's emergency room, holding a plastic bag.
It's cooler in here than on the street; a fever isn't as noticeable outside as it is in a cool hallway.

I wish someone would ask me something.

The hallway is freshly painted, but in this lighting it's a sinister shade of green.
The plastic bag holds Father's clean underwear, some pill bottles, his slippers and salesman class ring, and his bottom dentures. An old woman lies on a gurney. Brown leather shoes poke out from under her blanket. A young woman, a daughter like me, stands by the gurney holding the old woman's hand. They're both drying their eyes with tissues.
I want to be with my father, holding his hand and wiping my eyes with a tissue.

A door opens.
The smell of gruel, urine, and blood assaults her nose.

And

the surprising, offensive smell soothes her: her hours of feverish, aimless wandering have ended with her here, among instruments, IV fluids, the scuffing sound of Berkemann shoes, properly filled-out forms, and smells that assure her life will go on.

A nurse walks out into the hallway.
The nurse also has a bag in her hand. But her bag reeks: Father's dirty underwear is in it.
"What do you want to do with these?" the nurse asks.
I'm alarmed by this question that requires an immediate decision, and I wish the nurse would understand that I've just come back from a trip abroad and have a high fever.
"With what?" I ask, trying to buy some time to think straight.
"Aren't you with this elderly gentleman?"
"Yes, I am," I answer briskly, looking for understanding in the nurse's eyes.
"This is his underwear."
And the nurse lifts the stinking bag toward my nose.
I wave my hand carelessly in the air, and now it comes: a smile that starts by gently pulling at the nurse's cheeks and only then reaches her lips and eyes.
And

they burst into the laughter of two middle-aged people who are still going strong; they laugh at the stinking bag and the frailty that hasn't caught up to them yet but that they can sense nearby.

"What was it all for?"

Father was already struggling to walk, but he didn't yet have a cane.

We were in the tram on our way to Elsa's student recital at the Sibelius Academy.

Mother had promised to buy Elsa a piano when she turned five.

I'd asked for a piano when I was a child, but since Father no longer received a salary from the Finland–Soviet Union Society and Mother's salary alone had to cover food and rent, Mother taught me to sing instead.

Mother died before Elsa turned two, and Father remarried and forgot all about Mother's promise.

When Elsa turned five, I bought her a piano, explaining to Father that children had to have everything these days.

"That's true," Father agreed. "I didn't have anything when I was her age."

Neither did I, I wanted to add, but I adjusted my sentence so it sounded less accusatory:

"No one splurged on kids in the '50s either."

Father conceded I was right, and for a moment we drifted together in the barren landscape of a fragile but heartening solidarity.

Father held on to the tram's seat back with his good hand
and sat down with a soft thump.

"What was it all for?" he repeated.

"What's that?" I asked.

"That job I had delivering newspapers."

Father talked about this more and more often as he grew
older.

He'd been eleven at the time, living with Grandma and
Grandpa at 10 Torkkelinkuja lane.

Grandma worked at the Arabia factory, and Grandpa
was a lathe operator at a small workshop in the Kallio
neighborhood.

Grandpa used to drink back then, and people visited them
on Torkkelinkuja almost every night.

Father was in his first and only year at Kallio Secondary
School, and every morning at four o'clock, Grandma woke
him up while the last of the previous night's visitors lay
asleep sprawled across the floor.

Father had to go deliver the *Uusi Suomi* newspaper
downtown.

There was no tram service that early in the morning, which
meant Father had to run over a mile to Old Church Park,
where the papers were handed out to the delivery boys.

"It sure sleeted an awful lot back then," Father said, staring blankly out the tram window as we crossed over Long
Bridge. The Whites had bombed the bridge during the
Finnish Civil War, leaving gaping holes. "So what was it
all for?"

I sit in the hallway and wait.

The door to the room where they've taken Father is open.

It's eleven minutes to ten in the morning. A monotonous siren drones outside.

My fever is starting to go down; I'm sweaty and drowsy, and my heart beats unevenly.

I hear Father mumbling. He's asking for me.

Father's asking for me.

I get up and walk to the door.

The room is dark.

Room dividers separate the patients' beds.

Now it smells like vomit.

"Hey, Reiska," I call out randomly into the dark room.

Two people in white lab coats poke their heads out from behind one of the dividers. One of them is a young man with a mustache and the round, gold-rimmed glasses of an intellectual.

"Excuse me," I say.

I hear a moan from behind the divider. But it isn't Father.

"I am Reino Saisio's next of kin," I say loudly into the emptiness, but I immediately correct myself:

"I mean daughter."

Silence.

The white lab coats retreat behind their divider.

I remain on the threshold as a late blackbird chitters in complaint outside the window.

I step inside.

My shoes make a hollow sound on the floor. I write it as a sentence in my mind: *Her shoes clomped hollow on the floor*. I change the sentence: *Her shoes struck the floor, hollow*. I try again: *Her shoes echoed empty on the floor*.

I wipe the sentence from my mind and look behind another divider.

Father is there, looking back at me, but then his eyes roll back, revealing the whites.

"Hey Reiska," I say, taking Father by the hand.

Was she acting like a woman for the white lab coats who had reappeared from behind their divider, one of whom must be a doctor?

"Hey," Father says weakly. "So here we are."

"That's how it is," I say.

"Yeah," Father says. "Life."

"Yep."

"Just hanging on."

Father's hand rests in my own like a cold, reluctant fish.

I squeeze it, and Father tries to pull it away.

I won't let go; I hold on with the healthy, strong, and entitled grip of a family member and smile at the doctor.

"So can you tell me anything about his condition?" I ask.

"He seems tired," the doctor says.

Suddenly I feel weary, overwhelmingly bone-tired.

"Yes indeed," I say.

Someone cries out in the hallway.

The doctor and I both pretend not to notice.

"It's clear he needs to stay here," the doctor says, and I feel like crying in relief.
And

she wishes the doctor would see her: her fever and her fatigue and her senseless wandering out on the street.
But the doctor looks right past her to her father, who pulls his hand out of hers and rubs his cheek with his good hand like a child.

the fire

Grandma made me take lots of naps.
She believed sleep was the most important thing in the world for children.
And that adults should be allowed to drink their afternoon coffee in peace.

Grandma's the one who turned her into a daydreamer, by accident.

Grandma always pulled the curtains closed for naptime. The side facing the window, the side with the sun and Tepsi and the apple tree and her half-finished games, was brown with golden ears of oats.
The other side, facing the room and her tedious attempts to catch hold of her dreams, was gold with brown ears of oats.
Those curtains

later appear on a shelf in the walk-in-closet on Hämeentie road after her father's death, and the faint smell of camphor, flypaper, and a once-popular detergent makes her wistful.

She could hear voices behind the curtains.

Alf and the Alho brothers, who no longer had to take naps, were driving a wood pedal car out in the road. Mr. Viding had made it for Alf.

Grandpa didn't know how to make a car like that.

But he had built me a playhouse with a real porch.

It was painted the same green color found throughout their house: on the walls and the wooden floor grating, the benches and barrels, the dresser and dinner table, and whatever else needed paint to grace its surface.

That was the color you could get after the wars, Grandpa explained.

I lay there on the bedspread in the dark room, listening to Grandma sighing as she moved about the kitchen.

Grandma sighed a lot.

I can't sleep.

I'm anxious about when it will start growing.

Something pinches my stomach.

Maybe it's growing already.

Grandpa told me that if you swallow an apple stem, an apple tree will start growing in your stomach. Its branches will grow out of your ears and mouth.

"Will it make apples?" I asked.

"Well why wouldn't an apple tree make apples?" Grandpa replied.

"What apples?"

"What's that now?"

"What apples, what kind?"

"Well, Antonovkas for sure. And why not, White Transparents, too."

"Can you eat them?"

"I don't see why not."

"Can you pick the ones that come out of your ears?"

"Quit harping on about that already."

That was Grandma.

Grandma couldn't see the apple tree growing by the ladder from the kitchen window.

I'd reached for the lowest branch and managed to pick an unripe apple. I wasn't allowed to eat unripe apples, so I only ate the stem.

Nothing had happened by evening.

I touched my ears first thing in the morning. Nothing.

Grandpa had already gone to work, so I was forced to take up the issue with Grandma.

"How long does it take for a tree to grow?"

"What tree?"

"Well, an apple tree, say."

"Dear me, child," Grandma sighed. "Trees take a long time to grow. They grow slower than flowers or bushes, you know."

"But what if it's in your tummy?"

"What about your tummy?"

"What if it's growing in your tummy?"

"Why don't you go on outside and see what Tepsi is growling at," Grandma said. "Maybe someone's coming."

It's been two days now since I ate the stem.

I lie on the bedspread and wait.
I look at my hands. They're small and soft, and my palms sweat easily.

When I grow up and become a man, I'm going to get myself hands like Grandpa's: hands that are big and hard and dry.
Hands marked with welding burns.
Hands that can remove a crooked nail without a hammer.
And when

decades later she's grown into a woman and a mother—contrary to her intentions—she likes to look at the faded scars she's accumulated on her hands.

The curtains sway in a light breeze.
Two flies buzz around the ceiling light.
It's hot and I'm bored.
Grandma has put up a picture next to the framed photographs. She cut it out of a Finland–Czechoslovakia Society magazine and attached it to the wall using a cooked potato as a glue stick. It's a picture of workers in overalls gathering grapes in huge baskets.
I've eaten grapes once. Irja Markkanen sent some home from the store with Mother when no one wanted to buy them. They were small and sour.
I don't like grapes, and I don't like the picture either. It's blurry, and it's not even in color.
There's nothing else to look at in the room. Time stands still.

There is the wall hanging at the head of the bed behind me, I suppose.

But I don't like it, either.

Misse, the cat, has clawed the bottom edge to shreds, and it's almost completely worn through anyway.

It's supposed to depict Italy a long time ago.

It has grapes on it too, but more importantly, there's a little boy with a rope on it. The rope is attached to a stick, which holds up a box tipped upside down. The boy is smiling: a bird is just about to go under the box to eat some seeds.

"And then when the boy pulls on the string…well, that's it," Grandma once explained.

"That's what?"

"The bird gets trapped."

"What do you mean *trapped*?"

"The stick falls down, and the bird gets stuck underneath. Under the box. Oh dear, that poor little thing!"

"And the boy will gobble it right up," Grandpa interrupted her. "In those parts they'll eat anything. Starting with sparrows."

The apple tree still hasn't shown itself.

Time is slow, dusty, and dull.

Grandma opens the door.

I close my eyes quick and try to breathe evenly.

Grandma will ask me if I'm sleeping. I'm too smart to fall for that.

But Grandma is even smarter:

"Are you still awake?"

"No," I answer, and my face flushes red, before Grandma even has a chance to laugh.

But Grandma doesn't laugh.

"Get up," she pronounces solemnly.

I get up right away. I'm not sleepy at all.

I smell coffee in the kitchen. Tepsi rattles her chain in the yard and barks restlessly.

"Now sit down right there."

I quickly take a seat at the table. Grandma's voice frightens me. I run through the events of the previous days in my mind, but nothing stands out.

Except eating the apple stem.

"I only swallowed the stem," I say. "I didn't touch the unripe part at all."

But Grandma isn't listening.

"Look over there."

And the index finger Grandma broke while working at the Arabia factory points toward the window.

A field stretches out on the other side of the glass.

On the other side of the field hums the highway; it's the same road Mother, Aunt Ulla, and Father take to come here on Saturdays after the stores close.

And there along the edge of the field is a two-story building. It's the most handsome building in the whole area.

Everyone calls it Pikkatilly.

And

it isn't until forty years later that she happened to find out the building had housed a restaurant called

Piccadilly that was licensed to sell alcohol in the '50s.
Piccadilly was reopened in the '90s.
Apparently the renovated restaurant had photographs of the old Piccadilly up on its walls.
She decided to go look at the photographs but never got around to it.

Pikkatilly is in flames.
Flames leap high into the air black with smoke.
Fire trucks wail.
"It's burning down now," Grandma says, pouring coffee for us both. "What a pity."
"Is it going to come here?" I ask, suddenly anxious.
"What?"
"The fire."
"I doubt it," Grandma says, putting a sugar cube between her lips.
The room smells faintly of camphor. Grandma hasn't put any cardamom buns on the table, and I can understand why—fires are serious business.
"But will it?" I dare to ask again.
"What?"
"The fire," I say impatiently. "Will it come here? Over the field?"
"It won't."
And

only then can she bring herself to fully enjoy the moment. She wishes the flames would rise even higher, all the way up to the sky.

She wishes for more fire and more screaming sirens but less smoke.

Father played with matches once when he was a boy and caught the curtains on fire and got spanked right away.

I don't play with matches, but I still get spanked.

There's an awful story about a forest fire in a Donald Duck comic.

Alf and I don't know how to read, but we do know how to look at the pictures.

We see moose and birds and rabbits fleeing the red and yellow flames, and it makes us cry—Alf, too, even though he's a real boy.

We're sitting behind the spruce hedge, the lawn blazing blue with cornflowers and bird's-eye.

"What if there were a fire here?" Alf whispers, his lips trembling.

"What if Tepsi caught on fire?" I whisper back, and I can see Tepsi charging through the burning forest, her chain flying.

And suddenly, there on the other side of the field, the sky is burning, red and threatening.

Alf grabs my hand.

We stare at the horizon, terror stricken. Red flames swoop toward us across the field.

"It's over there," Alf whispers.

"I see it," I whisper back.

"It's coming this way!" Alf screams.

And he wets his pants, right where the buttons are, so I

know this is a life-or-death situation.

We smell the smoke in the air.

"We have to call for help," I say.

"Yes," Alf barely manages.

It's hard to call for help.

I open my mouth, only to muster a feeble whisper.

But Alf is braver and yells loudly:

"Help! Help! Helphelphelphelphelp!"

It sounds good, and this time I manage to yell just as loud:

"Help! Help! Help help help!"

We start running along the road, trying to outdo each other in our cries for help.

We forget the Donald Duck comic in the blazing blue field of flowers, and we never find it again.

Mrs. Viding comes runing out their gate, followed by Grandma running out our white-painted one.

Mrs. Johansson, our neighbor, peeks out from behind her lilac hedge.

"What is it?" Mrs. Viding calls from afar.

She's wearing a black beret. Her ears are scrunched down angrily under the sides.

Somehow the sight of the beret and the ears makes the fire die out.

"A fire," Alf tries, now in a normal, toneless voice.

"Where?" Grandma demands.

I look around.

The sky behind the field has turned a pale blue, and a wisp of a cloud trails over the spruce hedge.

"We were playing," Alf says.

"With matches?" Mrs. Viding demands. "You're never,

ever allowed to play with matches, not ever. You better remember that."

And she pulls Alf's hair for good measure.

She and Grandma have a brief consultation, even though they aren't on speaking terms, and they conclude we must've done something wrong.

After giving me a good spanking, Grandma sits me down at the kitchen table, places a butter eye bun and a cup of *viili* in front of me, and tells me a very serious story about a shepherd who kept yelling *a wolf is coming, a wolf is coming*, even though there was no wolf at all. Then one time the wolf really did show up, Grandma says, but when the shepherd yelled *a wolf is coming, a wolf is coming*, no one believed him anymore. And so the wolf ate all the sheep, though Grandma can't remember for sure if the wolf ate the shepherd, too.

I don't know what a shepherd is, but whatever it is, now I know you should never ever yell *a wolf is coming, a wolf is coming* unless there's a wolf in plain sight.

The most frightening picture I've ever seen of a fire is in the almanac with the brown cover that hangs from the same string as the copying pencil above Tepsi's bed. It's a drawing of children crying alongside the burned ruins of their home.

Grandma explains it's meant to be a lesson for children who like to play with matches, but Grandpa corrects her and says it's an advertisement for fire insurance devised by the bourgeoisie to collect money from poor people who own wooden homes.

None of the children in the picture have any burns, but the smallest child's teddy bear has lost an ear.

And the children don't have a home anymore.

They have no home at all.

When Grandpa comes home, I get to be the first one to tell him about the Pikkatilly fire because, even though Tepsi is the first to hear Grandpa approaching behind the hawthorn hedge, she's a dog and can't talk.

Tepsi grows restless before Grandpa even comes into view; she rushes to the kitchen door and starts scratching at it.

Tepsi and I run out to greet Grandpa.

Grandpa digs inside his briefcase and pulls out a piece of sausage for Tepsi and a Da Capo chocolate bar for me.

"Pikkatilly burned down," I say, but for some reason my voice is stuck in my throat, even though I've been preparing to say this all day.

"What's that?"

"Pikkatilly burned down today."

"So I heard," Grandpa says. He closes his briefcase, wipes the sweat from his brow with his rolled-up hat, and walks the rest of the way to the house in silence behind me and Tepsi, just like he usually does.

But Grandma and Grandpa talk about the Pikkatilly fire all evening.

Smoke rises from the ruins at the other end of the field.

The sun sets, and dark, ragged clouds sweep overhead.

We stare across the field, all three of us, as we eat Baltic herring with potatoes and brown sauce.

Tepsi begs at the table, even though she isn't supposed to, and Misse washes herself in the empty cake box on top of the dresser that serves as her bed.

"Looks like the fire department is still there," Grandma says, feeding potato peels to Tepsi.

"Why?" I dare to ask.

"They'll be there all night," Grandpa says.

"But why?" I try again.

Grandma takes the berry pudding from the stovetop and portions it out on the same plates we used to eat our potatoes, herring, and sauce.

At home we eat dinner and dessert on separate plates. Mother thinks eating dinner and dessert on the same plate is not only distasteful; it's plain old-fashioned.

"So why is the fire department staying there all night?" I ask, trying one last time.

"Stop fiddling with your glass," Grandma says. "Or that milk of yours'll end up all over the table."

We've talked so much about the Pikkatilly fire that the first star has already appeared in the night sky, and Grandma and Grandpa have forgotten all about my bedtime.

"Let's not say anything to your mother about this," Grandma says. "Or she'll start thinking we don't know how to take care of you."

We keep on talking about Pikkatilly in bed, the three of us, since we can't fall asleep.

But talking in bed is difficult because Grandma and Grandpa's dentures are soaking side by side on the dresser in the kitchen, and it's a little hard to understand what they're saying.

Grandpa smells of hand lotion and Grandma smells of camphor—it's been an especially rough day for her.

"And it's no wonder," Grandma says.

Grandma fingers the sheet she's crocheted with lace edges and embroidered with two red snakes. The snakes stand upright and twist and turn next to each other.

It's not until

she's an adult that she realizes the fiery red snakes stood for Grandma's initials: S.S., or Saima Saisio.

And it's even later that she remembers Grandma embroidered the sheets in the '10s when her and Grandpa's last name was still Sulander, before the wave of adopting Finnish last names in the '30s.

Maybe they chose Saisio as their last name so Grandma wouldn't have to unpick the letters she'd so carefully stitched into the fabric.

The sheets were made of thick, stiff linen.

She found them after Father's death, neatly ironed in the closet at Hämeentie.

She gave them all away, though she soon regretted her decision.

It was too late.

The sheets were scattered across the city: she found one separating the director's room from the auditorium at KOM theater in the Eira neighborhood a few weeks later and the other fluttering in the window of Rome Puppet Theater in the Vallila neighborhood the following spring.

"They were always making such a racket what with all the booze over there," Grandpa says in the dark.

Blackout curtains from the war years are pulled down behind the oat curtains; they're made of brown paper and badly torn.

I'm lying between Grandma and Grandpa on their double mesh-frame bed.

I'm pressed up against Grandpa because Grandma completely fills up her side of the bed.

"Police cars showed up practically every night," Grandma says.

"The wheels on the police car go round and round," I pipe up, but Grandma and Grandpa continue staring at the ceiling.

The smell of smoke has carried over the field; the wind must have changed direction.

Tepsi stirs restlessly. The smoke must be bothering her, too.

"The worst is what happened to that girl," Grandpa says.

"What girl?" I ask, but no one says anything for a long time.

"Just a few months old," Grandma finally says, her voice hoarse from holding back tears. "Oh that poor little thing!"

"So where did she go?" I ask.

"Burned to death, dear child," Grandma says, wiping her cheeks in the dark, hoping Grandpa won't notice and snap at her to stop sniveling in front of me. "Burned in her cradle. Or whatever they had over there."

Now she can't sleep.
She'd been waiting for this fire for so long.
She wanted it to happen—she's sure of it.
She wanted the flames and firemen and screeching sirens to interrupt her nap.
She'd wanted a fire, and she'd gotten one.
But she didn't want a child to burn to death.
Or

did I?

Grandma and I are still awake, even after Grandpa has turned on his side and started snoring.
Grandma gets up to eat a sandwich and take some camphor, and I get up to drink a glass of milk. My mouth is dry and my throat has almost swollen shut.
Then we lie awake some more.
Even Tepsi is awake. She sits up and stares at the smoking ruins through the window.
I don't know if I dare ask Grandma.
Grandma is unpredictable and easily provoked, at which point she goes outside to make a fresh switch of birch twigs and gets camphor from the dresser.
Grandma stares at the ceiling, sighing and secretly wiping her eyes.
I decide to try, carefully.
"Grandma."
"Yeah?"

"If you wanted a fire, well…"

She doesn't know how to go on.
She doesn't know what she wants to ask.
But she does know it's a matter of life and death.

"Well what?" Grandma asks hoarsely.
"Well, is it bad…?" I try at random.
"What?"
"To want a fire."
"For whom?" Grandma asks.

She's frustrated.
She didn't want a fire for anyone.
But she sure had wanted one.

"Nobody."
"Oh."
"They just wanted one."
"Wanted what?"
"Well, a fire."
"No one wants a fire," Grandma says.
"But what if someone does?"
"Does what?"
I don't see any point in going on, but I have to:
"Well what if a little girl wanted…a fire to maybe…
start somewhere," I say.
"That's impossible," Grandma interrupts. "That would
be a very bad girl. Downright mean."

Now her throat swells shut.

She would give anything, anything at all, never to have wished for the Pikkatilly fire.

She lies quietly in the dark.

If she confesses to Grandma, she'll get spanked right away, even though it's nighttime.

But that wouldn't be the worst of it.

Grandma would send her away.

Grandma would send me away.

Grandma would send me away if she knew what I was really like.

And after I'd been sent away, I wouldn't be able to find my way back to the city, because the conductor wouldn't let a downright mean little girl who wants fires on the bus.

I'd get lost in the forest and a wolf might come and eat me and no one would help, even if I yelled *a wolf is coming, a wolf is coming.*

Or maybe I'd come across a man in a trench coat and he'd force me to eat bad-tasting candy and do something that horrifies and excites me just thinking about it, even though I don't know what it is, because no one will tell me.

Tepsi would miss me. She'd whimper on her chain, not caring that I'd wanted a fire, because I'm the only one in the world who splits bags of Fazer's candy mix equally with her.

Mother would look for me, but when I couldn't be found, she'd go to Turto's milk store, where she got me, and get herself another baby.

The baby would be a girl and her name would be Pirkko and she'd have curly blonde hair and dimples, and she'd be good and obedient and cheerful. And soon Mother would forget all about me, so even if I managed to survive for days in the woods like Hansel and Gretel or those children from "The Birch and the Star," and even if I managed to find my way back to the city and my home on Fleminginkatu, Mother would no longer recognize me.

That became the longest week of her life.

Forty years later she could still see that pale little girl, listlessly loitering outside in the heat, flinging herself down on her back in the dry, prickly grass and staring at the burning blue sky trying to daydream.

But there wasn't a single shred of a cloud anywhere, and her thoughts turned heavy and empty.

Her eyes, burning from lying awake, drooped and closed. A plane droned above in the blue expanse of nothingness, and a persistent bumblebee buzzed by her ear.

Grandma woke her up there in the grass, by the well.

"You haven't been poking around the well there, have you?"

"No."

Grandma led her inside and sat her down at the table.

The brown field was visible through the window, and Pikkatilly's skeleton, charred black and glittering, stood behind it.

Grandma was angry.

And

as she looked at those two sitting on either side of the green table forty years later, she felt sorry for them both: for the little girl, whose guilt had made her depressed and mute, and for the old woman, who was alarmed by the little girl's sudden apathy.

The little girl vaguely understood that Grandma had been waiting for her throughout the dark and monotonous winter.

But she still didn't understand that Grandma was afraid of the summers that flew by so quickly, and of the winters that took the girl further away from her, year after year, as the girl grew older, more like an adult, more like a stranger.

Grandma often talked about how, once the girl was old enough to attend confirmation classes, she would give her a pair of blood-red ruby earrings; Grandma stowed them wrapped in newspaper in the dresser's uppermost drawer.

And

neither of us could have known that Grandma would die before I was confirmed, leaving the ruby earrings to languish in Father's walk-in closet in a bast-fiber basket for over thirty years until they suddenly appeared on

Kerttu's ears, only to disappear again in the timeless soundscape of the memory care home.

Grandma forced the little girl to eat some rhubarb soup and cardamom buns with butter, then lay her down for a nap in the room dimmed by the curtains covered in ripe ears of oats.
Grandma lay down too, and in a quiet voice, she told her three fairy tales in a row.

I didn't like Grandma's fairy tales.
In Grandma's fairy tales, the children were always selfish and often arrogant. And when the time came for bitter tears of regret, it was always too late.
Only cold embers or rotting crosses were around to witness the children's pointless pleas for forgiveness.
But

in Grandma's third fairy tale, the guilty party turned out to be a cat.
The cat knocked over a poor old woman's milk jug, and it made the old woman so angry she struck the cat. Offended, the cat disappeared into the darkness of the night.
The woman called for her cat, but the cat never came back, and so the woman wept bitter tears, first over the spilled milk, and then over her only friend who had left her forever and ever.
Grandma was weeping by the time she mentioned that the cat was the woman's only friend, and it brought

tears to the little girl's eyes, too.

First she and Grandma cried over the same thing: over the cat who was gone, forever and ever—and that cat was Misse of course, who at that very moment was probably contentedly washing herself in her empty cake box after having eaten an annoying squirrel she'd seen scampering about the apple tree all week.

And then they cried for their own reasons: the little girl because of her terrible guilt, and Grandma because her life had come to a standstill in a neighborhood as remote as Mellunkylä; and because she would never make it back to Kallio, where water flowed through pipes and you could pee in a porcelain chamber pot instead of a slop bucket and go to the market to buy fresh herring and eggs every day.

But even though Saturday seems an entire eternity away, it finally arrives after all.

Saturday is when Mother arrives.

I want to talk to Mother about the fire because I know Mother will be able to explain it away.

She's sure Mother will say no one would want a building to burn down, and by force of will, Mother will make her believe that, too.

I've picked a small basketful of strawberries for Mother from my own strawberry patch.

I only eat three while I wait for the BMW under the neighbor's's lilac hedge.

The BMW arrives in a cloud of dust, but even so, I can see Mother waving at me from the front seat.

Father brakes where I'm standing, and the back door opens.

Mother is freckled and beautiful and smells of the city, but I still feel calmer as I climb into the burning hot back seat.

Grandpa has started the fire in the sauna.

Now he's sitting on the green bench outside making sauna whisks.

Father plays with Tepsi.

Grandpa is upset because whenever Father is around Tepsi jumps and barks wildly and doesn't care about anyone but Father.

"What horseplay," Grandpa mutters, thrusting his cap farther back on his head. "Spoiling a good dog for no reason."

Grandma grinds the coffee on the front steps, and Mother sits next to her, absentmindedly popping strawberries into her mouth.

Mother is wearing her Bucharest Festival skirt. Father got it for her in Romania; the hem is lined with flattened globes around which the people of the world dance hand in hand hailing peace on Earth.

"It sure is nice to come out here after a rough week," Mother says.

"You all can go in the sauna first," Grandma says. "Then we'll have some good, strong coffee."

"Wonderful," Mother says.

Suddenly I'm anxious.

"No, let me go with Mother," I say, giving Mother the best pleading look I can muster.

"Isn't there room for your father?" Mother asks, not noticing my face.

Just then Tepsi's teeth slice a gash in Father's hand.

"These strawberries are so good," Mother says. "Reiska, try some, you'll see just how good they are."

"They're from my berry patch," I say.

"Is that so," Mother says in mock surprise.

I blush: Mother is such a bad actor when it comes to these things.

Father sits down by Mother's side, pressing a handkerchief to his hand.

"That dog should have been trained."

"No dog's gonna stand for that kind of horseplay," Grandpa says, and Father says what I know he's going to say:

"Well Taru, now, she was in a class of her own."

I hated Taru.

Taru was Tepsi's mother, and luckily she died before I was born.

There were albums full of photos of Taru.

Taru carrying a stick in her mouth and obediently looking straight at the camera.

Taru fetching a ball and Taru sitting on the sofa with her head cocked to the left, then on another sofa with her head cocked to the right.

Taru in a harness pulling a sled carrying a strange child

with blonde curly hair and a wool hat from the war years.

Taru's harness was still in the attic, but I had no intention of asking that it be put on Tepsi ever again.

Not after the time Grandpa, who always gave in to everything I asked for, had finally agreed to put it on her. Because while Grandpa was putting the harness on, Tepsi had tucked her tail between her legs, then ran around the yard whimpering.

"Well, why don't Pirkko and I go first then," Mother says, and I am grateful to her.

"Go on then," Father says, squeezing Mother's knee.

I notice Grandma look away.

Tepsi keeps licking her lips and glancing at Father.

In the sauna I have Mother all to myself.

I sit on the top bench next to her.

Mother is sweaty and pale and beautiful.

I need to talk about the fire, even though my skin burns and it hurts to breathe sitting up so high.

Mother throws a ladleful of water on the sauna stove and looks out the window; the view is of weeds and gravel.

Mother lies down on the bench, her head on my lap.

Her hair burns my thighs.

"Oh, it's so nice to be in the sauna," Mother sighs before humming a tune I don't recognize.

But

she could tell the song brought up memories for her mother that had nothing to do with her.

The memories were distant ones, and she felt a faint twinge of jealousy listening to the melancholy melody about times long ago and places far away.

"It's so nice to be in the sauna," Mother repeats. My sense of urgency is growing by the second.

"Guess what," I say.

It's a poor start; I realize it right away.

"Chicken butt," Mother says, lifting her legs straight up to the blackened ceiling.

"What?"

"Guess what, chicken butt," says Mother. "We always used to say things like that as kids."

"Oh," I say.

The stove hisses.

Fireweed pokes out of the tangle of weeds and taps against the blackened window.

Tepsi barks restlessly in the yard.

"It's so nice to be in the sauna," Mother says as she brushes her hands against her thighs and slowly wipes the sweat from her breasts and midriff. She sighs deeply and is gone, somewhere far away.

Mother and I sit on the bench outside wrapped in our towels, drinking juice made the previous summer.

The juice tastes more like mold than strawberries.

Father scrubs the hood of the BMW with a cotton cloth. He's wearing his driving cap, and every now and then he stops to look at his reflection in the hood. He thinks no one is looking.

Tepsi pretends to sleep, ignoring Father, whose hand Grandma has bandaged with fabric from an old sheet.

Grandpa squats down to cut the sun-scorched grass with a hand sickle.

"Has your grandpa already had something?" Mother asks me.

"Had what?"

"Booze," Mother says. "He sure is working that sickle fast."

Grandma opens the window.

"Are you coming?" Grandma calls through the curtains. "Coffee's just about ready."

Now I'm in a hurry.

"That fire," I say, even though Father is within earshot. Mother looks at Father, and again a fragment of a song wells up from her throat.

"What is it?" Mother asks, clearly distracted.

"The Pikkatilly fire," I say, freezing inside despite the warmth of the evening.

"Oh, that," Mother says dreamily as she smiles at Father, who has put his driving cap on the BMW's hood. "It was something awful."

The kitchen window opens again.

"No need to hurry," Grandma calls, leaning on the green windowsill. "Don't think that now. Take as much time as you like."

"Let's go back inside," Mother suggests, getting up from the bench and wrapping her towel more tightly around her. She breathes in deeply as a subtle chill rises in the darkening summer night.

"What a nice evening."

Mother shampoos my hair in the sauna.
It's hard to say anything in this position.
"It doesn't sting, does it?"
"No," I lie.
Mother pours a bucket of cool water over my head, and I'm done.
Then Mother starts washing her own hair.
I look at Mother, her beautiful body covered in a veil of foam.

Now's my last chance.

"Mother, listen," I say boldly.
My heart is beating so hard it hurts my ribs.
"Would you mind washing my back for me?" Mother asks.
I swallow my disappointment and wash my mother's pale back with a sponge.
"That sure feels good," Mother says. "It's so nice to be in the sauna."

We dry off and drink another glass of the strawberry juice that tastes like mold.
Mother combs her hair.

Mother's hair is dark and curly and short. She has a perm.

"All right," Mother says, content and absent. "Let's hang our towels on the line."

"It was my fault," I say quickly, looking at the untreated boards lining the sauna's walls.

"What was," Mother says, but I can tell she's gone, somewhere far away.

"The fire," I say.

And now Mother sees me; she really looks at me for the first time all evening.

"Who told you something like that?"

She pulls strands of hair from her comb before placing it on top of her dirty underwear.

"Was it Grandma?"

And

a chasm opens in her mind, leaving Grandma on the other side, alone.

It's never occurred to her that Grandma could do anything wrong.

It's never occurred to her that people could have different opinions about Grandma. Or about Father or Mother or Aunt Ulla.

Only her own actions were wrong or questionable—because she was a child.

And for a moment she feels tempted to give up, to claim Grandma had been blaming her for the fire by ignoring her and crying and lecturing her with disturbing fairy tales all week.

Mother waits, and she wavers.
But the thought of a new layer of guilt brings a hesitant confession.
"No."
Mother's eyes bore through her, and

how ugly she is standing there.
How naked she is, in her own eyes.

"Well who then?"
"I did," I say, placing the burden on myself once again.
Mother laughs in relief as she puts on a pair of clean, pink panties and a bra that's also clean and pink.
The bra's hooks fasten into the eyes naturally and gracefully.
Mother's breasts slip obediently into the cups,
and

she's jealous of her mother and her dreamy content-ment, the casual femininity from which she knows she will forever be excluded.

"Now how could it be your fault?" Mother asks gently, buttoning up her festival skirt.
"Well, I wanted it to happen," I manage to say, even though I can sense my defeat as I'm confessing.
"You wanted what?"
"The fire," I say, utterly worn out.
She hears Grandma's footsteps outside,
and

she finally gives up: she gathers her dirty clothes, puts them under her arm, and turns to go when Mother suddenly understands, takes her in her arms, and holds her close.

There they stand on the floor grating, Mother breathing into her wet hair, and Mother's heart beating against her forehead.

And even though it's the first time Mother feels like a stranger, she doesn't want to let go of this moment, this embrace

and I never did.

dream colors

The path is a silver, winding string that leads to a house where no one lives.

It's midnight. She stands on the path, about to enter the house illuminated by the moon.

The lilacs are in full bloom, and the deserted home is practically drowning in their blue plenitude.

The yard is overgrown with pansies.

They even poke through cracks in the walls.

She opens the door, and it creaks dryly.

No one's inside.

Strange white curtains flutter in the windows.

There's an empty white bowl on the table, menacing pansies blooming on its surface.

A teapot on a shelf has pansies poking out of its spout.

The night screams emptiness as she stands alone in this house illuminated by the moon, and when she turns, she finds the doorway choked with pansies: a deep, cold, blue.

Then she wakes up.

She's tucked in bed under a gray-and-blue-striped soldier's blanket.

The lights are off in the aquarium she's been ordered to watch to help her fall asleep. Fish sway to and fro in the green-tinged emptiness.

The blue abandoned house has enchanted her: she's never seen anything as blue as she has in this dream, in the depths of this landscape of death.

And she's never experienced a loneliness as perfect as that of the dream house's vacant, mesmerizing blue.

She's four years old at the time, and she needs to talk to Mother about it.

But Mother is sitting at a table with other adults.

Mother is visiting this place, just as she is, and the table is brimming with youthful exuberance, outbursts of laughter, snippets of song, passionate debates, and clouds of cigarette smoke rising in thick swirls.

She fights against sleep. She's afraid she'll end up in the dream house again.

But as the voices at the table mix with the clattering of the last tram, she sinks back into oblivion.

Now she's walking hand in hand with Father along an empty cobblestone street.

It's night, and the moon is shining wickedly again.

The last tram passes without stopping to open its doors, even when Father hits its thunder-gray sides with his fist.

They're forced to continue on foot.

They're forced to lose their way.

The cobblestone street deadends at the edge of a forest.

It's foggy in the gloom, and the moon's icy glow reflects off the bare treetrunks.

A blueish-black pond lies deep in the woods, and there under its frost-covered surface appears a woman's face.
The woman's eyes are open, and all you can see under the surface is her head, cut off but alive.
The head sprouts enormous pansy petals shaded in midnight blue.

She forgot this dream for thirty years, but then it suddenly returned, not as a nightmare but rather a harrowing image that tormented her for months as she teetered on the verge of sleep.
She'd been abandoned then, and the past and the future unfurled around her like the desolate Russian steppes.

She often dreams in blue and learns to seek out its unconditional loneliness.
During the day she longs for the deep blue of her dreams, but she only finds pale fragments: a fair summer sky; a field of bird's-eye; a mop of cornflowers deep in a ditch; the window frames painted blue when Porkkala peninsula was leased to the Soviet Union.
And she persists in dressing solely in blue for nearly thirty years: jeans, sailor's shirts, and captain's coats; shirts in the familiar Russian blue and scarves the color of blue flames.
In Bangladesh she bought a blazing blue scarf from a rickshaw driver who'd been wearing it around his neck, only to discover at home that the scarf needed the last tired rays of the southern sun to shine.

Even her Mexican shirt and Greek vest lost their blue sheen in Finland's pale winters.

Red is no color for dreams.
Red is the color of deception—she learns that early.

When Mother and Aunt Ulla spread rouge on their lips, they become inexplicably excited, and you can't believe the promises that slip out of their painted lips.
When Grandma repots her red peony, fall is well on its way, even though Grandma tries to convince herself and the peony that summer will go on.
And the family brings Grandma a red amaryllis when she's in the hospital and there's no more hope. They talk about the amaryllis all through the visiting period, about how Grandma can take the amaryllis home and plant it in one of the flowerbeds in summer where it will keep making flowers throughout the season.

And when she makes love to a woman for the first time, the room may have green walls and a plastic orange ceiling light from the '70s, but their love won't last long. Because the room's true color is scarlet.

She only has one red dream.
She's in another house, also empty.
But this house belongs to someone, and she knows she has no right to be there.
She goes inside anyway, she can't explain why, not even in her dream.

She wanders through the rooms, opening drawers that aren't her own; reading a letter addressed to another; sitting on a chair that's still warm; looking, stroking, and touching things that belong to someone else.

There's a TV by the door with a red porcelain hand on top. There's a window above the hand, its blackout curtain raised.

She stumbles over a shoe, and the shoe makes her realize someone is coming.

She tries to run away, but her movements turn slow, involuntary, like glue.

She's almost at the door when the red porcelain hand reaches for the string holding the curtain and rips it down.

She likes brown dreams.

In her brown dream she's in front of a community center.

It's nighttime again, and the moon is out.

Men in black coats and Borsalino hats move about the yard with expressionless faces—later she will be delighted to recognize them in Magritte's surrealist paintings.

Grandpa's in the yard, too.

He's also wearing a black coat and a black Borsalino, and he drinks liquor straight from the mouth of a blazing-blue bottle.

But Grandpa has on brown corduroy pants underneath his black coat, and she leans her cheek against the fabric.

His pants smell of tar, decaying algae, and the sea.

Brown is the color of homemade malt beer, rust, barges, and chocolate: the monotonous familiarity of everyday life.
She likes rust.
Rust softens the crosses in the churchyard and makes doors creak cozily.
The rough specks of rust on a hunting knife temper its pompous posturing.
Rust's brown shades reveal the past and the future all at once.
Brown reeds are no longer alive but not yet dead.
Brown is the comforting color of gradual death.

There's a house in her gray dream, too.
It's a pearly gray, two-story wooden home, surrounded by birches sparkling with frost.
It's a wet, cloudy day, and she's an adult.
She's about to step inside, a rain-drenched, charcoal cloak draped over her shoulders.
She stops at the door when she sees two silvery porcelain poodles on the windowsill.
Dew drips from her mustache—yes, in this childhood dream she has a mustache gracefully turning gray!
But she never gets to go inside, because this softly shining pearl of a dream is meant for the open air, spun from sorrow, lucidity, and tomorrow.

Yellow is a boring color.
Yellow is endless sunshine; Easter, afternoons, and egg

yolks; an audacious lily that dares to poke through the snow even though it will begin to droop before spring has even properly begun.

She's only had one yellow dream, and in it, the yellow was soft and sacral, shaded with the colors of fall.
She was in Barcelona, well into middle age, and she had a fever.
She swayed between waking and sleeping in the bed of her small hotel room when the church bells in the plaza started ringing.
The heavy tolling of the bells entered her dream, and suddenly she was swept into Millet's *The Angelus*.
She stood between the two peasants with their heads bowed, smelled the earth and the pungent odor of sweat, and marveled at the cool calm of the golden valley in the setting sun.
The peasants exchanged words in another language.
She didn't understand the words, but she carefully touched the woman, felt the coarse dusty fabric at her fingertips and the sunburned stubble beneath her feet.
The intense sensations evoked by the dream stayed with her throughout the following afternoon when she and her traveling companion discovered a small stone castle on the Catalonian highlands.
It turns out Salvador Dalí had had it built, and he spent twenty years of his life there.
And the dishes, linens, towels, and fountain tiles—they were all decorated with variations of Millet's *The Angelus*.

.

miss lunova

We go to the Linnanmäki amusement park every summer.
All six of us go: Mother and Father, Grandma and
Grandpa, Aunt Ulla and me.

We arrive early, in the afternoon, so that Grandpa and I
can ride the ghost train before the Green Branch Revue
at the Peacock Theater.

I'm not afraid of ghosts, just as I'm not afraid of the
dark or of being alone.

The ghosts remind me of the clowns in the Green
Branch Revue. They look funny and smell of dust,
woodchips, and engine oil.

None of the things I'm really afraid of are on the ghost
train, like hair salons, photography studios, clothing
stores, or the women in blue-checked dresses who blow
their whistles when it's time to go stand in line at the
playground.

And there aren't any feathers either.

I'm afraid of feathers most of all. They crawl out from
the pillows at night, and in the morning they protrude
in the air, mean and prickly.

But there is a No. 3 tram on the ghost train.

It suddenly rushes around a corner to run over you,
and

the tram from the ghost train enters her dreams. She
has nightmares about trams for the rest of her life.

Grandpa and I also go in the Mermaid House.
There's something strange about it: people laugh at
those who go inside.
At first I think the adults are laughing at me, but to my
disappointment I realize everyone except Grandma is
laughing at Grandpa.
And somehow their laughter is connected to those
nights when Grandpa doesn't come home and Grandma
cries all night long.
But

no one else knows about Grandma's crying but her, and
that's why she squeezes Grandma's hand before she joins
Grandpa and walks between the clumsily painted mermaids at the door, entering into the smoke and noise.

Mermaids in swimsuits sit on raised seats behind chain-
link fencing.
Grandpa and the other men throw tennis balls at them.
If the ball hits the right spot, the seat gives way, and the
mermaid falls shrieking into the water.
The smell of sweat, smoke, and liquor fills the air, and
whenever one of the mermaids falls, everyone bursts out
laughing.

I feel sorry for the mermaids.

I understand the shrieking is a part of the game, but each time a mermaid rises to the surface, her mascara running down her cheeks, she doesn't even try to fake a smile.

And something strange and frightening happens to Grandpa in the Mermaid House.

Grandpa clenches his jaw and gets a hard look in his eyes as he takes aim.

And if the ball misses its target, Grandpa swears, quietly and intensely:

"Goddamn…"

I'm relieved when we're back outside in the sunshine and the fresh air, and when I thrust my hand into Grandpa's, he becomes himself again.

"All right then."

I don't like the wheel of fortune either because I feel sorry for the adults who feel sorry for me unless I win something. I usually do win something anyway, like a teddy bear or a key ring with a two-tone plastic whistle; that's because Aunt Ulla keeps feeding it money until the quivering pointer stops on the number one of us has selected.
And

even though she's only five years old, she vaguely understands that her aunt is the only adult who isn't playing for her, but for herself—and later her aunt instills the same passion for gambling in her.

Initially they make bets on trivial things: Will the next car to pass be green or black? Will the first animated film at the variety show theater be *Tom and Jerry* or *Donald Duck*? Will the evening's radio announcer be Carl-Erik Creutz or Kaisu Puuska-Joki?

Later they play card games like Old Maid or Musta Maija for pocket change.

They switch to casino and then to poker; they raise the stakes from coins to bills.

She and her aunt share a lottery subscription for over fifteen years, and Aunt Ulla sends her many chain letters promising hefty sums of money.

She and her aunt play quinella, first at the Käpylä racetrack and later at Vermo Arena.

And she and her aunt stand together at the first legal roulette table in Helsinki.

As the croupier gathers the chips from the baize, her aunt—who has advanced pancreatic cancer but is warmed by two Irish coffees and their shared gambling habit—asks her to pick up the hand-painted plates of game birds she's ordered from Hobby Hall if she dies before the last one, due in a year and a half, can be sent to her.

Of course she will, she says, and for the rest of her life she will treasure the words her aunt, stacking more chips on the table, mouths with her red lips:

"I should have known even without asking that, of all our relatives, you'd be the one I could count on to take care of this."

Linnanmäki has all kinds of things I don't like. Take cotton candy.

It's pink and girly and disappears.

I refuse to go on the swing ride, even though that's the ride all the other children want to go on. At least all the fun-loving children do, so says Father.

I have to go on the animal carousel because it's the only ride Grandma will agree to go on.

Grandma sits on one of the carousel's benches eating ice cream.

I'm lifted onto a giraffe or a horse, and Grandma holds on to my ankle so I won't fall off.

Going around the carousel makes me feel queasy, but I can't bring myself to say anything.

I do like the Green Branch Revue, though.

I get to sit on someone's lap and watch the performance in peace.

The Green Branch Revue is why I look forward to going to Linnanmäki all summer.

And now

the day has arrived.

They walk along Helsinginkatu, where they can hear the faint screams from the roller coaster.

The street swirls with the dust of August heat, and the little girl, who's been forced to wear a blue floral-print dress and a blue silk bow, looks like a sheepdog trying to keep her flock together.

But the two men, one young and one old, have gotten far ahead: the old man wears a cap, and his hands, idle as Sunday, are clasped behind his back. The young man has his coat thrown over his shoulder, holding it by the crook of a finger, and smokes a cigarette, carefree and dapper.

The little girl catches up to them, thrusts her fingers into the old man's dry hand, and tries to slow him down.

The sisters, wearing red lipstick and high heels, walk far behind the men, whispering with their heads together, and an old, sweaty woman waddles behind them, swinging her sizeable black purse for momentum.

The sisters are the first to stop and make room for the panting little girl as she thrusts her hands into the sisters' cool ones with the red-painted fingernails.

The old woman reaches them and opens her purse to take out a neatly ironed green-striped handkerchief; she wipes the sweat from her neck and forehead.

And the little girl generously removes a hand from its cool refuge and places it in the old woman's sweaty one. She doesn't want her grandmother to think she's forgotten her or her lesson: she won't be the little girl left alone in the cemetery, full of pointless regret.

Usually everyone starts talking about the Green Branch Revue while we're still on Helsinginkatu, but this time the adults tell me about someone I've never heard of before, a person named Hitler.

I gather that Hitler is dead but that his terrible deeds live on.

Even his name is terrifying. It's as sharp as a razor, a blunt threat, and nothing at all like the names Lenin, Stalin, or Kekkonen, which sound like gently lapping waves.

Father says there's an article in *Työkansan Sanomat* that describes everything Hitler's henchmen did to little Jewish boys and girls.

I don't know what a henchman is, but it doesn't seem appropriate to ask Father about it now, since everyone else seems to know what it means and is hanging on Father's every word with horror and disgust.

Father says there was a henchman who stopped a little Jewish boy on the street and asked him to take a letter to the other side of town, to a Mr. So and So at a sausage factory. The little boy ran through the city and handed the letter to the appropriate Mr. So and So, not suspecting a thing. Mr. So and So opened the letter and read that he should make sausage out of the courier because the boy was a Jew.

The Jewish boy was fed into a sausage machine, and the sausage was sold to bourgeois German housewives at a butcher shop for a good price.

Her legs no longer want to carry her.

But no one notices because she keeps on walking.

She feels a strong urge to ask something, but she doesn't know what.

So she keeps on walking, even though the asphalt sinks beneath her feet like soft cotton, the sounds of the roller coaster fade away, and the sun grows dark.

I could be that little Jewish boy.

And she refuses to go on the carousel, even though Grandma is already sitting on a bench with an ice cream cone in hand.

She won't ride the ghost train or play the wheel of fortune either.

The adults form a wall around her; they beg and plead and try to bribe her; they feel her forehead, which is both hot and cool.

Mother fixes her sad, drooping silk bow; she looks away, senses something, and hums a melody, releasing it into the gloomy air.

I want to go home.

I want to be in the alcove, in the dark. I want to be in the dark alcove so I can come up with a way to save the little Jewish boy.

It could go like this: The boy opens the envelope, even though he's not supposed to, and reads the letter inside. He runs home and shows the letter to his father, who gets angry and takes the letter to the police. The police are just as angry, and they shut down the sausage factory.

Or it could go like this: The little boy gives the letter to Mr. So and So, and he opens it. He tries to grab the little boy, but he escapes. Mr. So and So stumbles on the sausage machine, falls into it, and is ground to death.

My head and stomach hurt by the time the Green

Branch Revue begins.

I sit on Mother's lap, even though Father says I'm too big for Mother to see properly.

In a whisper I ask Mother when the show will end, even though it hasn't yet started.

Mother whispers back and asks me to try to sit still, at least a little while, for everyone's sake.

I try.

But the sausage machine pulses before my eyes, its cogwheels grinding little girls and boys to bits, leaving nothing behind but a blue hair ribbon for someone to send to their mother.

Until Miss Lunova steps on stage.

Miss Lunova announces when each performance will start.

She makes her announcements by stepping on stage in a swimsuit.

In her hands she carries a heart-shaped poster with a number on it.

She takes a few steps in her high heels, looks at the number, and feigning confusion, turns the poster around. The other side is covered in writing.

I can't read it, but I guess it says the name of the next performer.

Miss Lunova is the most beautiful woman I've ever seen.

She's stunning.

Mysterious.
A foreigner.

Miss Lunova has black hair and red lips.

Miss Lunova is a Jew.

I'm sure Miss Lunova is a Jew, but I turn to ask Mother just to be sure.
"Yes, yes," Mother whispers. "Now let's be quiet, so we don't interrupt the show."

I don't care about the show.
I don't care about the magic tricks or even the clowns.
I just wait for Miss Lunova to appear.
And

suddenly she realizes what love is.
She loves Miss Lunova.

Up until that point in her life, Grandma is the only person who has ever used the word *love*.
Mother and Father talk about *liking* someone.
Grandma tells her she must love her mother and God and Father and Grandma and nature and Grandpa and her country and her neighbors and being obedient.
Love is an order and an obligation.
But now her love has nothing to do with obligations or expectations.
She loves Miss Lunova with a passion that consumes

her, and she doesn't have time to be scared or hope for anything until the final curtain is lowered.

But

when the curtain falls, she's suddenly frightened.

And her fear is just as hot and all-consuming as her love: she realizes she has lost Miss Lunova for good.

But she refuses to believe it, and she decides to fight for her love.

I want Miss Lunova to move in with us.

Miss Lunova has to move in with us because I can't live without her.

And Miss Lunova can't live without me.

I can't sleep that night. My body aches because I'm at home while Miss Lunova is somewhere else.

And I know Miss Lunova can't sleep either—because I'm not by her side.

I don't dare say anything until the morning. I'm at the Teboil station with Father getting gas for the BMW.

I try to speak in a normal voice, but it comes out tense.

"Miss Lunova is moving in with us."

Father starts the car and pushes down the cigarette lighter.

"Let's stop by Markkanen's store."

"Miss Lunova is moving in with us," I say. "She has to."

"I'll get some OKA coffee," Father says. "You can get yourself a new trading card."
I start crying.
Father doesn't notice.

But Mother does, and Father finally does, too, because I cry the entire evening.
"What the hell has gotten into her now," Father says.
"Miss Lunova is moving in with us!" I scream. "She has to!"
Mother and Father look at each other in surprise.
I can see it through my veil of tears, and I feel sorry for Mother and Father, because they don't understand me.
But I feel even more sorry for Miss Lunova, who is a Jew and whom I can't save.
"She's an adult," Mother begins carefully. "She has her own life, dear child."
And it's only now

that she understands the situation in all its cruelty.
She will never get to have Miss Lunova.
Miss Lunova will never get to have her.
She will have to forget Miss Lunova, and to her horror she realizes that is exactly what will happen.
But the most horrific thing of all is that she will never get Mother and Father back, because they don't understand any of this.

a.p. chekhov's idle days

Father was in his shirtsleeves, the elastic sleeve garters pushing the loose folds up to his biceps.

It was early September, and there was a late heat wave. The crepe-soled shoes she'd gotten for school left saw-toothed impressions in the soft asphalt.

Father dropped a cardboard box in the middle of the floor and wiped the sweat from his brow with his sleeve.

"Take a look. See if there's anything there. I'll take the rest down to the basement."

I opened the cardboard box.

It wasn't full of bananas.

Two weeks ago Mother had brought home a box of bananas from Markkanen's store; they were covered in brown spots and too soft to be sold.

We ate bananas for three days straight: with morning coffee, with lunch, and with evening coffee. I couldn't eat bananas for a good while after.

Now the box was full of books.

I'd learned to read late that winter, and with shaking hands I began to unpack the box.

But there wasn't a single book by Anni Polva, Enid Blyton, or Astrid Lindgren.

The writers had names like A. Tolstoy, V. Kataev, Galina Nikolaeva, M. Gorky, Belyaev, Lysenko, and A.P. Chekhov, and the names of the books were just as strange: *The Lone White Sail*; *Workers' Stories*; *Firestorm*; *Introduction to Genetics*; *Stories and Selected Stories*; *The Lady with the Dog and Other Stories*.

Disappointed, I let Father take the books down to the basement. I wouldn't fetch the box until we'd moved to the neighborhood of Puotila, and Mother and I had carried all forty-eight volumes of Lenin's and Stalin's *Collected Works* to the trash one night, leaving the mahogany veneer shelf deserted.

And even though Chekhov's *The Lady with the Dog and Other Stories* smelled bad—it had been printed in the Karelian Autonomous Soviet Socialist Republic where all books smelled like that—and the pages had yellowed over the past five years, I read it, and

to her surprise, she smells fresh lilacs and a currant leaf warmed by the sun—and there's the distant smell of thyme, even though she has no idea what thyme is;

she hears a dog's stubborn barking, full of sorrow; the distant hum of telephone lines; and an intense, discordant thwack as if a cable has snapped somewhere;

she sees the dizzying blue sky and a dark cloud in the shape of an anvil forming in the distance, and she feels

the burning sun and the capricious breeze promising thunder on her skin.
Because

this Chekhov, this writer I don't know, has unexpectedly plunged me into an idle villa life long forgotten.
But the language spoken there isn't Russian, and the people whiling away the afternoon aren't dressed in white summer outfits buttoned up to their necks; no one drinks champagne or eats sturgeon or white fish; no one goes horseback riding or plays the guitar.
Still, the sorrow—the sorrow is the same.
Even though no one sits on wicker chairs on the lawn but rather on soldier's blankets brought down from the attic; even though no one is offered wide-brimmed white hats under which to while away the afternoon—if rhubarb leaves aren't large enough to protect their heads, they're given scarves and hats stowed in Grandma's entryway instead;
even though no one lounging on the blankets next to the turnip beds is discussing gulls, the centuries, the glory of work, or the future of humankind—
still, the drowsily buzzing bees and dragonflies are all the same.
As is the brewing thunderstorm and the restless rustling of the birches' leathery leaves,
the denial of fall's impending approach and the fear of a long, snowy winter.
But

the copper coffeepot steams on the green stool brought out from the sauna as Mother's uncle puts a lilac leaf he's wet with spit on Aunt Martta's burned nose.

Aunt Martta is roused from her torpor; she lights a cigarette and coughs violently.

"Damn this weather."

And Grandma says: "Girl, go get some juice from the basement. Put as much in the pitcher as I've showed you and then top it off with water from the bucket."

She stays in the basement for a long time, in the cool humidity that smells of dirt and cement.

She's been blinded by the sun, and it's hard for her eyes to adjust to the dim light; the objects gradually begin to take shape on her retinas as dark, shapeless lumps: the chopping block and the pile of wood that smells of birch, the bow saw and the cement bin filled with potatoes sprouting blue-gray shoots.

There's a pile of sawdust next to the potato bin, and deep below the sawdust is a block of ice that was hacked out of the sea in winter.

She puts her hand on the block of ice, keeps it there until her hand grows numb.

She presses her cheek against the cement wall covered in gray frost. Pleasurable shivers run down her spine.

And when she goes back outside with the pitcher of juice, the familiar question is waiting for her:

"What on earth took you so long?"

The mood has changed; she senses it clearly and is alarmed.

Time no longer stands still. It gallops ahead like the black clouds now releasing their first heavy drops of rain.

Everything's whisked inside: the coffee cups and coffeepot; the crystal sugar bowl and its protruding sugar tongs that resemble hawk talons; the creamer without a handle; the butter eye buns and the blankets.

And the inevitable moment when someone glances at their watch is at hand, threatening the peaceful Sunday on the porch that's suddenly grown dark.

"What are you in such a hurry for?" Grandma asks dejectedly, even though she knows the answer.

"It's back to work in the morning."

Because

they aren't in one of Chekhov's *Selected Stories* after all, but in the middle of 1950s Finland, and from that yard in Mellunkylä her family will be off to rebuild Finland: they'll toil in a textile factory, lay asphalt, and cut hair; they'll print books, make Fazer candy, and help in a grocery store; they'll build Solifer generators and work in the Department of Film Propaganda at the Finland–Soviet Union Society.

"The weekend will come around again," someone says, trying to comfort me and Grandma.

Then we notice a barn swallow teaching its chicks to fly in the rain.

"Already?"

That's Grandma.

"Well, that tells you summer is just about over."
And that's Grandma's sister Kaisa.

Grandma and I don't want our visitors to leave, because a long week of empty days lies ahead of us, waiting for Grandpa to come home from work in the evening. Grandma is worried I won't enjoy myself, and I'm worried Grandma will think I'm not enjoying myself and start crying as a result.

Sometimes Grandma lies down on the bed on her side and cries all day long, about things that are none of my business (dear child) or anyone else's for that matter.

Then I lie down next to Grandma, and I cry too, for so long I get bored.

Then I get up and grab myself some viili, which itself turns weepy when a thunderstorm threatens; I eat it and go outside to wait for Grandpa with Tepsi.

Tepsi wags her tail a few times when she sees me, but then she yawns and puts her muzzle between her paws; she closes her eyes and sinks into a dispirited sleep.

And

with nothing to do, she loiters in the yard, then climbs up the ladder to look through the window to see if Grandma has gotten up or fallen asleep.

If Grandma is on her back and snoring, she climbs all the way up to the roof.

The felt roofing burns the bottom of her feet and smells like tar, but she can see far from up there.

She can see the bay full of reeds and a neglected boat

tipped on its side; it's the very same boat her family used to take on fun trips to Tapiola and Mustikkamaa, before the bay turned shallow and she was born and Grandma gained weight and got depressed.

She can see Pikkatilly's ruins and the humming highway and the Vainios' house, where a woman was murdered with an axe.

She can see Bomann's store and the pharmacy, and she can almost make out the Elanto co-op, known for its good bread and bad meat.

Through the heat she can see the burned fields, a lonely cow flicking its tail, and a runaway dog happily pausing to sniff in the ditches.

Grandma and I spend a lot of time sitting at the table and staring at the road, always at the road.

We're waiting.

The waiting is the worst every other Saturday.

That's Grandpa's payday.

When I'm little, Grandma often says:

"I wonder if he'll come home at all."

And when I'm bigger, it's me who says:

"I wonder if he'll come home at all."

And Grandma says:

"That's no concern of yours, dear child."

Grandpa ought to show up at the hawthorn hedge around one, since the factory's whistle blows at twelve.

If Grandpa comes home at two, three, or four in the afternoon, Grandma doesn't even bother to look angry.

If Grandpa comes home at five or six, he's sure to be tottering unsteadily on his feet.

Grandma looks angry then, but she calmly tells me to take Tepsi and go make sure Grandpa can make it to the door.

And Tepsi and I run out to greet Grandpa.

When I'm bigger still, I'm on Grandma's side, and I try to look angry, too, but Grandpa doesn't care. He takes a piece of sausage for Tepsi and a bag of liquor-filled chocolates for me from his briefcase, where he keeps his thermos, then pinches my nose and chuckles happily:

"There's my girl."

Grandpa comes in behind me and Tepsi and hands over his earnings to Grandma, and she puts the money in the dresser without a word.

Grandpa sits down at the table, takes a bottle of Karhu Vodka out of his briefcase, and puts it on the floor by one of the table legs.

"Tell her to get me a glass out of the cupboard," Grandpa instructs me.

"Get him a glass out of the cupboard," I tell Grandma, and Grandma says:

"Tell him to get it himself."

There are also those Saturdays when Grandpa doesn't come home until after midnight. Or worst of all, not until Sunday afternoon.

I sleep on Grandpa's side of the bed, since Grandpa doesn't have any business in his bed on those nights.

The all-request show on the radio is long over, and

Grandma has asked me to go to sleep at least ten times. Shadows get tangled in the spruce hedge.

Grandma gets a few sugar cubes moistened with camphor, and I stare at the brown stains spread across the ceiling, the result of water damage from long ago.

And as she stares at the stains, she tries to grab hold of a thought she realizes is both important and frightening.

Everyone likes Grandma and Grandpa, but it's only Grandpa that people tell stories about.

The stories are about Grandpa's youth, when Grandpa was a flyweight boxer and a handsome, well-dressed man. He had stiff collars and snug-fitting suits; he wore ties and shiny shoes.

In these stories Grandpa appears on dance floors, in Kappeli restaurant in Esplanadi Park, or else in shady salons that have something to do with prohibition and half-naked women.

And there's a woman in one story in which Grandpa is already a father. Grandma's asked Grandpa to walk up and down Porthaninkatu with the stroller carrying my tiny, sleeping father, while she stays home on Pengerkatu to cook dinner.

The woman comes across Grandpa by chance, and Grandpa politely lifts his Borsalino to the woman and then quickly pushes the stroller under an archway.

Then there's a break in the story lasting a few hours, and it doesn't pick back up until Grandpa remembers to get the stroller with Father from under the archway and go home for dinner.

People tell this story often, and Grandpa blushes but chuckles happily every time, while Grandma goes to another room to check on something.

No one seems to notice Grandma.

And the thought she's still too little to understand as she stares at the stains on the ceiling only becomes clear to her as an adult: people still considered Grandpa a man, but Grandma was no longer considered a woman.

And then Grandpa arrives.

Tepsi barks inquiringly; she dashes to the kitchen door and scratches it.

She frantically circles the kitchen and even paws at the bedroom door.

But both doors stay closed because Grandma has decided they will.

Grandpa stumbles on the threshold, muttering:

"*Herkele…*"

He must be cursing the threshold and not Tepsi since he talks to Tepsi for a good while after, feeding her sausage and setting my bag of liquor-filled chocolates on the table.

I hear the crinkling sound of the bag—I can hear it clearly through the door—but I can't bring myself to climb over Grandma to get my treat.

"He's been drinking," I whisper to Grandma.

"Shhh. Let's just listen and see what he does."

He looks for something to eat in the pantry, but he stumbles again, and one of the chairs falls to the floor. Tepsi barks wildly.

Grandma wipes her eyes, and I grow anxious, until I notice that Grandma is laughing so hard her blanket is jiggling.

And I start laughing under Grandpa's blanket until it starts jiggling, too, as tears stream from my eyes.

"Oh, that man," Grandma sighs. "Now let's see what he gets up to next."

Grandpa gets up to eating something and going outside, but he stumbles on the very same threshold.

And again:

"Herkele."

Koski Hl., in the province of Häme, is the one place in the world where people curse by saying *herkele* instead of *perkele* like the rest of us.

Or they'll say things like: "He won't amount to nothin'."

Or: "When a man can't even put a hat on his head."

Or: "Nothing's gonna come of it. Mark my words."

Or: "I can drink you out of house and home."

Grandpa came from Koski Hl., just like many of the people who showed up at the hawthorn hedge on the weekends.

Grandpa had two kinds of relatives: those who were dead and those who came to visit.

And he had two kinds of dead relatives: those who left a photograph behind and those who only left stories behind.

She felt closer to those who'd only left stories behind than she did to those who'd posed in their Sunday finery in some studio long ago and now stared blankly back at her.

Grandpa's mother was unbelievably skinny and wrinkled, and even as a five year old, she could tell her great-grandmother was wearing the checkered blouse with the white cuffs and the ironed pinafore for the first time in the photograph.

But Grandpa's stories didn't make her feel any closer to her great-grandmother. Her great-grandmother refused to give up her stiff, stern stare until a mysterious incident forty years later blew the breath of life into her nostrils.

There weren't any photographs of Grandpa's father, since he died before his children had earned enough to afford going to a photography studio.

And so in her mind her great-grandfather appeared alive and powerful at his table as he ate his bread and meat with a *puukko*.

Ten barefoot children swarmed around him, six of whom would die of hunger and disease before reaching adulthood.

Her great-grandfather shooed his children away like

flies, but if any food was left over, he'd throw a piece up in the air and laugh heartily as his children fought over it.

Great-Grandfather couldn't stand his youngest son, Nestor, her grandpa. Nestor was smart and foul-mouthed, which to her surprise means the same thing as having a sharp tongue.

The last straw came when Great-Grandfather, chasing him with a birch switch, fell flat on his face in a goose-berry bush while Grandpa jumped over it and escaped.

Coincidently she finds herself standing in that same yard forty years later.

Nothing is left of the cabin: not a single pane of glass or a section of cornerstone, not even a single twisted nail.

The fireweed, pale and exposed, shivers in the March cold where the cabin once stood, which had really been nothing more than a tenant farmer's sagging, dilapi-dated hut.

She's had to come all this way to realize there never was any gooseberry bush growing in the yard.

But this realization doesn't stop her from picturing Grandpa lunging over a thorny bush, wild and proud.

After the incident with the gooseberry bush, Great-Grandfather vowed to kill his son with an axe if he ever laid eyes on him again.

Grandpa wasn't worried in the least, but Grandpa's emaciated mother was. She sent her son into hiding at her mother-in-law's.

Grandpa was cold and hungry but comfortable at his grandmother's place, where his grandmother would gladly have talked to him if there had been anything to talk about.

Frost flowers bloomed on either side of the cabin's only window, and together he and his grandmother watched the landowners ride their sleighs to Christmas Mass through the frosted glass.

His grandmother couldn't provide for him though, and since no one else was willing to take him in, Grandpa was sold as a farmhand when he was only seven years old. Over the next five years Grandpa got to see the homes of many landowners.

Some were good, and some were bad.

In the good homes, the master and his family ate the same food together with their workers. In the bad ones, the master and his family only pretended to eat and then withdrew to their bedrooms to rest and eat what people are supposed to eat: butter, oatmeal, and meat.

But Grandpa's life wasn't all bad in Koski Hl.

Working as a farmhand, he got to know a group of boys who were related to us somehow; they were his first or second cousins.

Coincidentally, there were seven of them altogether, and they didn't have a mother, father, or master to give them any trouble.

They went fishing and hunting whenever they liked, taking Grandpa with them.

Grandpa even attended the same itinerant school with

the boys, but they weren't the learning type. This made the parish clerk angry, and one time he locked them up in the schoolroom as punishment.

But the boys took out their lunch sacks and swung them around a few times—and there went the school windows!

When he was twelve, Grandpa ran away to Helsinki to work for his brother Vihtori.

Vihtori was a handsome, greedy man with a mustache, and in the space of a few years, he'd managed to buy two horses, father six children, and get a permit to drive a horse-drawn cab.

Grandpa would drive Vihtori's cab around town, evading the police and the gentlemen in their silk hats, as he wasn't legally allowed to drive a cab until he turned fifteen.

After a few years, Grandpa had filled his pockets with a small fortune from driving the cab, and he was ready to plant his feet under his own table.

But then Vihtori up and died, and Grandpa suddenly had six underage nieces and nephews to provide for.

These children had grown into big, boisterous adults by the time I was a child.

I liked Aunt Maiju best.

You could hear her voice long before she rounded the hawthorn hedge, where she appeared in a black hat with a ribbon that looked like a pair of perky squirrel ears.

Maiju was big and happy and always yelling. She was so scatterbrained she never seemed to notice me.

She was so scatterbrained in fact that she once went to the Finnish National Opera in her house slippers when Uncle Yrjö arranged a complimentary ticket for her.

Uncle Yrjö wasn't a member of the family, and no one liked him, even though everyone admired and respected him.

Uncle Yrjö always wore a bowtie, and if he and I happened to be out in the yard together at the same time, he quickly turned his head away, since he didn't know what to say to children; I felt sorry for Uncle Yrjö, who hummed songs that weren't pop songs or even Russian battle songs.

A doorman at the Finnish National Opera, Uncle Yrjö sat in his apartment on Sundays with the curtains closed, listening to operas and ballets on his raspy turntable, even though the sun was shining and our relatives and other normal people were outside skiing or training dogs.

Uncle Yrjö married Father's cousin Aunt Sirkka twice, and divorced her the same number of times.

Aunt Sirkka was a hairdresser who'd cut Uncle Yrjö's black, curly hair, and told us about him for years before they were married the first time.

Everyone said Uncle Yrjö was a handsome and proper man, and when he showed up at Grandma's the first time carrying a bouquet of flowers and wearing shiny leather shoes, no one could disagree.

No one disagreed either when, after their first divorce, Aunt Sirkka said Uncle Yrjö was the coldest, meanest person who'd ever sat in her salon chair.

Aunt Sirkka had a goiter, which is why she had such big, protruding eyes and was so restless she might visit three people the same evening, unless she happened to be married to Uncle Yrjö.

In the mid-'50s, Aunt Sirkka starts visiting us on Fleminginkatu twice a week, on Tuesdays and Thursdays. She's now married to Uncle Yrjö for the second time.

Mother wonders about her regular visits, but she always makes coffee for Aunt Sirkka.

Aunt Sirkka drinks her coffee standing up and starts playing The Star of Africa board game with me, but she stops in the middle if she happens to glance at her watch:

"Oh my…look at the time… I better get going…"

And without finishing her sentence, Aunt Sirkka puts on her coat and slips on her shoes. As soon as the door closes, the doorbell rings, and Mother slips Aunt Sirkka's glove through the crack in the door before the door closes again.

And

most of the winter passes before Aunt Sirkka shows Mother what she has in her purse.

It's a pair of ballet shoes.

But another winter passes before Uncle Yrjö finds out his wife isn't going to ballet classes on Tuesdays and Thursdays as they'd agreed.
And they divorce, again.

Father and Grandma and Mother and I think it's a good thing when Uncle Yrjö leaves the family.
Uncle Yrjö may be a handsome and proper man, but he doesn't know how to act like regular people do.

Grandpa's foster children do. When they're sitting at the coffee table or sprawled on their backs or their sides in the grass after the sauna, a bottle of Karhu Vodka lying empty by their side, they carry on like this:
"Herkele, I built a house."
"What is it you built?"
"I built myself a house, herkele."
"Oh yeah? I can drink you right out of your house."

Grandpa looks shy and slim next to his foster children. She feels sorry for Grandpa because no one seems to remember that he's the father and master of his house.
His foster children lift him in the air and wrap him in their arms, and the old flyweight boxer disappears in huge, suffocating hugs.
They drink him under the table, and after Grandpa has passed out in the yard after working too hard to heat the sauna and acting too much like a man, Aunt Maiju lifts him onto her back and carries him off to bed.

But Aunt Hilma and Aunt Helmi think Grandpa is a manly man, even though he's their little brother.

Aunt Hilma and Aunt Helmi usually arrive at the hawthorn hedge together, because they moved into a studio apartment together on Ensimmäinen linja street after they both became widows.

They walk slowly because Aunt Hilma limps.

Aunt Hilma also has a deep scar on her cheek because one of Grandpa's brothers, who later died of hunger, hit Aunt Hilma in the face with a rock when she was just a toddler under the nonexistent gooseberry bush.

Aunt Helmi swings a purse in each hand; one is hers, and the other is Aunt Hilma's.

I sit on Aunt Hilma's lap. Aunt Hilma likes me because her son Reino—called Big Reiska to distinguish him from my father, Little Reiska—is divorced, and his ex-wife has custody of their two sons, which means Aunt Hilma has room in her heart for a bad, dark-haired grandniece like me.

I take Aunt Hilma to my playhouse despite Grandma's protests, but due to her ailing leg, she can't sit down on the stool and remains standing by the playhouse door.

And there by the door Aunt Hilma admires her brother Nestor, my grandpa, who is so good with his hands that he was able to build a playhouse for someone as small and insignificant as me.

Aunt Helmi doesn't care much for children, especially not an only child who's bad and dark-haired like me.

Aunt Helmi has first two and then ultimately five grandchildren of her own.

She and Grandma go to the Ruoholahti neighborhood to take care of her little second cousins when their father is working and their mother is traveling.

Her cousins are smaller than she is, pale, and drool so much she gravitates toward the edge of the stove where Grandma, Aunt Hilma, and Aunt Helmi stand together drinking their coffee, taking turns wiping their eyes with the corner of a dirty tea towel.

They talk in whispers, repeating the word *Hämeenlinna*, and based on the tone of their voices, she knows they aren't talking about Hämeenlinna being Grandma's hometown.

Her cousins' mother is gone for over half a year, and she knows not to ask Grandma why, not even when it's just the two of them.

When the Pollaris show up at the hawthorn hedge, she's afraid she'll be exposed, and so she thrusts her hands in her pockets and spits casually, looking indifferent.

She doesn't run up to greet the Pollaris, because Uncle Tauno and Aunt Kaarina are inevitably followed by Helena.

Helena is my second cousin.

Helena is my best friend—or I'd like her to be.

Helena has blonde, curly hair and dimples.

And

she's already learned this:

Blondes are good and brunettes are bad, especially if they happen to be girls.

Blondes are always good in fairy tales, and almost always so in real life.

In fairy tales and pop songs there's always one girl with light hair and one with dark hair.

They're often sisters with a widowed mother, but not always.

In fairy tales, the blonde is usually a princess, and the brunette is her mean and jealous stepsister.

The blonde has a harder life than the brunette, at first, but in the end, everything turns out well for her.

The brunette laughs in the beginning but dies in the end.

Her own hair grew darker by the day.

Since her hair was dark, she was inherently bad.

It might be worth trying to be good, but ultimately, any such attempts were bound to fail.

People with dark hair never get anything in life for free.

Having dark hair was fate, just like being an only child was.

I eat the half-melted ice cream Aunt Kaarina has brought, painfully aware of each wasted minute, but I still don't dare look at Helena.

But Grandma notices my anguish and tells us to go outside and play, just Helena and me.

I hang back, waiting for Grandma to tell us to go outside again, and when she does, I get up and shrug my shoulders indifferently.

"If you say so."

I take Helena to the strawberry patch; it's my very own patch.

I pick the biggest, ripest strawberries, the berries I've saved just for her, and put them in her hand.

Helena smiles and absentmindedly places them in her mouth—it's just the kind of treatment blondes get all the time.

And

before the burning sting of our separation, when I'll go up to the attic to cry on my own, we have a long, idle afternoon ahead of us, one that I anxiously and jealously guard.

The sun shines as if I were blonde and it were my ally, and Helena shows me how to find faces, animals, houses, and cities in the puffy clouds.

And just as Helena begins to grow tired of watching the clouds, rain—the natural ally of brunettes—starts to fall and I take Helena to my playhouse where I get to be the man of the house.

Helena sits on the only stool, of course, and I sit on the floor, feverishly trying to think of something to say, something that will force Helena's distracted, wandering gaze onto me.

When I do say something, Helena laughs politely, and I turn red with rage.

I'm furious at myself for boring Helena.

I want to *be* Helena with her blonde hair and dimples, who's distracted and bored in a friendly way, but instead I'm small and dark-haired and jealous of Helena's thoughts, and it's not until Helena is gone that I can go up to the attic and imagine the afternoon differently: I'm a boy and I'm tall and in third grade, my hands covered in welding scars.

Helena has fallen and torn her skirt. I pick her up and comfort her; I dry her cheeks with my scarred hands.

No.

I'm a boy and I'm tall and I'm in third grade.

I'm on a walk with Helena when a rabid German shepherd dashes toward us; its muzzle is black like Taru's.

It's about to attack Helena when I lunge between them and the dog bites my hand instead, but I don't cry; I tell Helena to run, and she dashes off to tell Grandpa. And Grandpa comes and saves me and…

No.

I'm a boy and I'm tall and I'm in third grade.

I'm on a walk with Helena when a rabid German shepherd dashes toward us; its muzzle is black like Taru's.

It's about to attack Helena when I lunge between them and the dog bites my neck and I die and I'm buried in Malmi Cemetery under a marble gravestone. Helena cries at my grave and…

No.

I'm…

I'm myself and I'm on a walk with Helena when we come across a German shepherd and…

No.

I've gotten all I can from the German shepherd, and Helena's face begins to disappear even though she only left a few hours ago.

I'm forced

to be small and bad and dark-haired again, a girl with chubby hands.

I'm forced to sit alone in the attic, to smell the dust and the light, unroasted coffee beans Grandma is saving for the next war in case of another coffee shortage.

I'm forced into everyday life, even though it's still Sunday evening—Grandpa is chopping firewood while Grandma takes the slop bucket to the compost heap.

I'm forced

into tomorrow where I'm not a boy after all, but I can read.

I grow closer to the people in the stories printed in the Karelian Autonomous Soviet Socialist Republic—later I will discover they were invented by Chekhov—than I am to the people I live with.

I don't understand the connection between *herkele* and Koski Hl. until Väinö Linna introduces me to his characters from the same area in his *Under the North Star* trilogy.

But even characters like Preeti Leppänen and Aune, or the violent Anttoo and the tormented Alina, don't show the kind of misery I see in my great-grandmother's photograph.

She's thin, so unbelievably thin and downtrodden, and I don't know her name.

There's nothing in her expression, not even suffering: no sign of life or fear.

The stories I hear about her aren't about her at all but rather about the circumstances in which she lived.

This woman, without whom I wouldn't exist, remains a mute stranger to me

until

an absurd coincidence brings her to a stand of alders on a frosty March afternoon when she's a plump, middle-aged professor.

The fireweed shivers, pale and exposed in this spot where her family's home once shivered in the cold: it was a tenant farmer's sagging, dilapidated hut.

She's ashamed of her nostalgic crusade to her family's birthplace, and she's ready to go home when she's given a surprising gift.

It comes from a woman who is the only person still alive who knew her great-grandmother.

The woman wipes her nose, reddened by the wind, on her knitted wool mitten and says:

"She didn't have an oven or anything. She only had an upright wood-burning stove, and she used it to cook whatever she had. But then in the '20s, when her kids who'd survived had grown up and moved to Helsinki for work, she started to prosper. She started making cardamom buns every Saturday after her kids sent her money for the flour. But since she didn't have an oven, she'd let the dough rise at her place, right here, and then she'd come over to our place to bake them, in my mother's oven. That's where she baked those buns of hers."

And now

I've got her.

My great-grandmother walks down the road in the baking summer heat, the fall slush, and the gleaming frost of winter, carefully carrying her covered tray of buns in her gnarled hands from one Saturday to the next, one week to the next, and one year to the next. For all of time.

rubies; forbidden love

Miss Lunova had dark hair.

Aira Hokkanen, my first teacher, had hair that was nearly as dark.

Mother's hair is curly, permed, and almost black.

But Mother's eyes are blue.

Even darkness has its limits, but Aunt Martta far exceeds them.

Aunt Martta not only has black hair, she has black eyebrows and eyes the color of coal.

Her gaze is black and penetrating, which is why no one likes Aunt Martta, not even me.

But Aunt Martta isn't part of the family, so we don't have to like her.

Aunt Martta is my great-uncle's mistress, and there's something wolflike about her: it's in her frightening gaze and the way she pants from smoking and gets hotheaded about every possible thing.

But the worst thing about Aunt Martta is that she doesn't let my great-uncle finish telling his own stories.

My great-uncle is called Väiski, or Uncle Väiski.

Uncle Väiski is everything Aunt Martta is not: he's Grandma's brother and a real relative; an easy-going, quiet, sensible person.

Boats have played a special role in Uncle Väiski's life, even though he comes from the interior, just like Grandma does.

Uncle Väiski knew how to make the finest toy boats imaginable when he was still in Hämeenlinna, which Aunt Martta describes to us even though she was just a baby swinging in a cradle clear on the other side of Finland.

When he was nine years old, Uncle Väiski moved with his parents and sisters, Grandma and Aunt Kaisa, to Kallio.

Uncle Väiski was bored at school, carving sailboats into his desk with his penknife, fervently longing to grow up so he could go live at sea; so says Aunt Martta, who was wearing a bib at the time and learning to eat oatmeal with a spoon.

Uncle Väiski's father provided for the family by keeping the public sewers clean, and he agreed to let Grandma stop going to school after fourth grade so she could go sell herring with Aunt Siiri at Hakaniemi's outdoor market. But he expected more from his only son.

And so Uncle Väiski had to go on sweating at his desk until his father died of gas poisoning in Helsinki's sewers.

Aunt Kaisa and Grandma were so upset by their father's death that they joined the Salvation Army—but Uncle

Väiski was more than ready to head out to sea.

And he did, as prisoner aboard a ship called the *Nautilus*, which transported Red prisoners to the Suomenlinna prison camp.

At seventeen years old, Uncle Väiski had joined the Red Guards, only a few days before General Mannerheim and the Whites arrived in Helsinki.

Aunt Martta described the prison camp in vivid detail and at great length: the streams of hopeless prisoners, their faces ashen like a desolate fall sky, or clay, or dead reeds; the screams at night when fathers were taken out to be executed; the mute earth wearied by the volume of innocent blood spilt; the helpless hands rising out of the poorly covered mass graves, proof of humanity's ugliest crimes; the endless, monotonous moaning of the sea accompanied by screeching gulls.

"But you weren't there," Aunt Essu interrupted, throwing Reea a tennis ball.

Reea was Tepsi's puppy, a well-trained one at that, and she easily caught the ball in the air. Tepsi, who'd never been trained, jumped, too, barking helplessly.

"You were just a little girl back then."

That was Svenkka, Aunt Essu's husband, leaning against a birch tree with an old soldier's cap on his head.

Aunt Martta looked at Svenkka with startled black eyes. "Well heck, a person can use their imagination, can't they?"

Svenkka laughed the way you do at someone who

doesn't understand a thing, and she, five years old, laughed with him.

Everyone knew that making things up was the same as lying.

At least Aunt Martta didn't cut in to describe Uncle Väiski's return from prison, since there was an eye witness for that occasion: Grandma.

Grandma was at Hakaniemi's outdoor market selling potatoes with Aunt Siiri (no one expected any herring in those hard times) when an unrecognizably thin young man hobbled up to them and presented himself with his given name of Väinö, Grandma's brother.

Grandma and Aunt Siiri filled Uncle Väiski's cap with potatoes and told him to go boil them in Aunt Siiri's apartment on Viides Linja.

But then Aunt Martta, coughing violently, described how it took Uncle Väiski two hours to hobble up Porthaninmäki hill: he had to stop at times to lean against a wall, and in the end he crawled the remaining distance on all fours like a dog.

Uncle Väiski ate the potatoes till he passed out and was fixing to die for a whole week before Grandma and Aunt Siiri were able to revive him.

Then he went out to sea again, this time as a cook.

And Uncle Väiski sailed to Rio de Janeiro and Havana and Buenos Aires before meeting Aunt Martta and getting a job working in public utilities, following in his father's footsteps.

Aunt Martta was a widow—her husband Artturi had died just like a respectable smuggler of moonshine ought to.

Aunt Martta vividly described the police interrogation during which the pale and profusely sweating Artturi was strip-searched. Artturi wiped cold sweat from his brow first once, then again, with the handkerchief Aunt Martta had washed and starched for him. The second wipe was followed by a terrific bang, and the policemen were knocked backward, some to the floor, others into the table. And when the officers recovered and stood up, Artturi lay slumped in his chair, his temple spurting a terrifying amount of blood.

It so happened that Aunt Martta's washed and starched handkerchief had hidden a revolver.

But because Artturi is even less of a relation than Aunt Martta, we don't really care to hear more about him, and instead we ask Uncle Väiski to tell us more tales from life at sea.

Uncle Väiski is a lazy and lackluster storyteller, but after a few sips of cut brandy, he's willing to give it a go.

Uncle Väiski's stories are full of monkeys, parrots, and large, threatening men.

But when Uncle Väiski tells us how a huge man with a knife pursued him through Kingston, we can't picture the city before us.

It's night—Uncle Väiski does remember to mention that—but the night is neither stiflingly hot nor cool, neither cloudy nor clear. The night isn't quiet, but there's no sound of cicadas trilling in Kingston's trees either, no distant sound of a guitar or the heavy breathing of Uncle Väiski's pursuer. And the rhododendrons, which Uncle Väiski does mention, have no smell until Aunt Martta gradually gets involved in the story.

Aunt Martta stealthily slips a rose between the teeth of Uncle Väiski's pursuer. A bottle of rum appears in Uncle Väiski's hand, and he valiantly refuses to let so much as a single drop fall to the ground. A few incredibly large raindrops fall, cooling Uncle Väiski's forehead. There's the distant bray of a donkey and the ghostlike echo of heels clicking on pavement; a red lantern in the window of a narrow alleyway; a one-eyed stray dog standing by an open door; and a military officer stroking his mustache, his boots gleaming in the night.

And Aunt Martta takes over, lingering in the lights and smells, the twists and turns of the plot; she builds the suspense before finally bringing the story to its blood-curdling conclusion.

We don't press Uncle Väiski to marry Aunt Martta—even though it isn't exactly appropriate for them to live together out of wedlock—because we secretly hope Uncle Väiski will find a softer, quieter partner, someone whose teeth are a little less sharp and who will let Uncle Väiski finish his own stories.

But Uncle Väiski unexpectedly proposes to Aunt Martta

at the end of the '50s, and Aunt Martta unexpectedly
says yes.

Aunt Essu and Svenkka loan their rings to the bride
and groom, and Aunt Martta goes to Aunt Sirkka's
salon to get her hair done.

With her hair curled and the borrowed rings in her
pocket, Aunt Martta dutifully waits for Uncle Väiski
and her bouquet of roses in front of the courthouse; she
waits an hour and then another before she goes home to
move the two single beds to opposite sides of the room
again, where they will remain for the next thirty years.

Uncle Väiski, who went out drinking on his wedding
day, proposes to Aunt Martta many more times, but she
remains fiercely inflexible.

As a teenager, when she was endlessly tormented by
a halfhearted, unfocused desire to rebel, she started
visiting Aunt Martta and Uncle Väiski in their studio
apartment.

She was intrigued by Aunt Martta's wolf-like gaze, and
even though she felt weak and strangely insignificant in
her aunt's fiery, unbending presence, she secretly hoped
that she, too, would turn into a wolf under her aunt's
influence.

And

to her relatives she praised Aunt Martta's story-tell-
ing gifts, her psychological perception, and her highly
developed aesthetic sensitivity; she was moved by her
own words (a trap she constantly falls into throughout

her life) and achieved the desired effect: her relatives' faces flamed red with rage.

She used words with foreign origins like "psychology" and "aesthetics" to cut herself off from her family; she left everyone behind and took only Aunt Martta with her, who was merely an ordinary worker at a printing plant and at best distinguished herself from the family through her endless chatter, her all-around snobbery, and the stealthy ways she hid her drinking.

It's a Monday afternoon, and as I sit in Uncle Väiski's and Aunt Martta's only armchair, I float above the noise of Helsinginkatu's long-haul trucks and my endless church history homework brimming with Gezeliuses and Rothoviuses.

Uncle Väiski is in the kitchenette making coffee and sandwiches on French bread smeared thick with butter and topped with bologna. Aunt Martta says no one butters bread as carefully or spreads cold cuts as evenly as my uncle and the Danes renowned for their Danish sandwiches do.

Aunt Martta sits upright on a wooden stool, inhaling her Klubi cigarettes; she uses one to light the next and is absorbed in the world of gemstones:

The white sapphire is a pure, delicate stone, reminiscent of a twinflower sparkling with dew.

It suits women who are young and frail and who don't yet know where life will lead them. A white sapphire glows at a young woman's neck, hinting at vague promises should a ray of light happen to touch it.

And on a summer night full of meaning, in the translucent coolness of dusk, the white sapphire bursts open to reveal its singular, soft light, the significance of which only those with wounded hearts can appreciate.

Aunt Martta glances at me, and I understand that Aunt Martta has a wounded heart, just like I will, in time.

And yet we aren't white sapphire women, Aunt Martta and I.

The diamond is a hard, confident gemstone.

It suits jealous women who advance through their lives proud and erect, never asking permission from anyone.

Again Aunt Martta glances at me, and she smiles a little; we're getting closer to the gemstone that suits us both.

But the diamond is too straightforward, too superior and brilliant. We reject it with a weak smile.

Aunt Martta does have some advice for those who would like to wear diamonds: make sure your eyes blaze as proudly and confidently as the gemstone you wear; pale and insecure women are no match for diamonds.

Turquoise may look opaque, but it's a steadfast stone that conceals the secrets of Native Americans and other indigenous peoples and reflects the placid depths of the Mediterranean Sea.

Turquoise suits women who have a heavy burden to carry but don't want to show it; instead they hide their greatest sorrows deep within their hearts, weighed down by everyday toil.

Amethyst sparkles with dazzling brilliance and the restlessness of a mountain stream.

It encapsulates the properties of running water in search of its depths, which is why it suits women who feel water's urgent restlessness in their souls.

But the ruby is the most wondrous of them all.

The ruby glows with the fire of passionate, inescapable love, and it only suits women who brazenly throw themselves into the hot and treacherous throes of lust, ready to bear the consequences of their bold actions for the rest of their lives.

And now Aunt Martta looks

at her.

The gaze unnerves her, because the woman's eyes undress her and uncover the hot, insecure, and and as yet shapeless mass at the core of her being that she's so painstakingly worked to conceal.

And that's not all.

Her aunt looks through her to the place she's just beginning to move toward, to the place she may never wish to reach.

One of Aunt Martta's legs was amputated before she was separated from Uncle Väiski for good.

I held Aunt Martta's hand in Helsinki Surgical Hospital, in the run-down hallway decorated with woodcarvings.

Her black wolf eyes were open, her pupils constricted in pain, and she was panting.

I cried out of fear and self-pity; I didn't want to be left alone in a world where no one saw me.

My tears fell on Aunt Martta's hand, and stirring, she

trained her hot and terrified gaze on me without seeing me. "My leg's gone. Ah well. It was a good one."

Aunt Martta ended up in assisted living, and she lay in bed for four years waiting for the atomic bomb to blow the world to pieces because Uncle Väiski had not been admitted to the same facility.

"They have no right to live together, or even to demand something like that. At the end of the day, they were nothing more than strangers to each other."

That was Aunt Sirkka, whose gentle but protruding eyes maliciously roved across the floral wallpaper, seeking revenge.

And it's only now that

she understands what a threat Martta's and Väinö's strange and silly love must have been to Aunt Sirkka, a woman who had twice been in love and twice been rejected—and to anyone who was afraid their inconsolable loneliness would be exposed.

swallows are bad birds

Starlings are nice birds.

They flit through the trees and pick tufts of fur from the air, glossy feathers glinting.

When the first starlings appear, Grandma gets Tepsi's brush from the dresser. We go out in the yard, Grandma and I, and we brush out Tepsi's winter coat.

Grandma flicks a tuft of fur into the air, and a starling skillfully nabs it in its beak and carries it off to build its nest.

The starling lays its eggs in Tepsi's fur, and Tepsi's fur warms the newly hatched chicks.

After we finish brushing Tepsi, we put her back on her chain; otherwise she'll try to chase the tufts of fur and get her coat back.

Starlings are good birds, because their arrival marks the start of summer.

Grandma never talks about death at the beginning of summer, not even the summer when she comes home from Maria Hospital to recover from an operation.

"Grandma's home," she says, patting Tepsi on the head.

"Everything's all right again."

Tepsi sniffs Grandma cautiously.

Is it Tepsi's timidity that made her suddenly realize this was to be the last summer of her childhood?

Swallows are bad birds.

The first one shows up and settles on a telephone line on an ordinary August day. Soon, another swallow will perch next to it, and before you know it, there'll be a whole row of them.

They look like a uniform string of black pearls.

The first day, Grandma and I might pretend not to notice them.

But by the second or third day, Grandma is bound to say: "Looks like the swallows are flocking."

I hate flocking swallows, because it means my parents will soon pick me up in the BMW and take me back to the city.

"Ah well, there goes another summer," Grandma says, and if I don't get myself out of the kitchen, and fast, I'll end up in Malmi Cemetery in a time when I've graduated from high school and grown so conceited I don't even remember Grandma and her lessons.

I sit in my playhouse, which suddenly feels small and strange and autumnal.

Maija and Pipsa lean against one of the walls.

Sawdust leaks out of Maija's fingers and she smells bad, but I still regret that I didn't take her out into the fresh air all summer.

I take both dolls into the yard.

There they sit under the black currant bushes, smiling their lifeless smiles.

I go sit on the front steps.

Tepsi comes up to lick my knees, and that's when I start crying.

Grandpa thinks I must not be happy at home because I cry for days on end leading up to my parents' arrival.

He even suggests I move in permanently with him and Grandma.

Though not in my presence.

I don't hear about it until I'm behind the curtain in the alcove, back in the city, when Mother and Father think I'm sleeping and start discussing the matter.

Mother is crying, saying she's done everything she could, but now Grandpa thinks she's such a horrible mother that even her own child doesn't want to live with her.

I'd like to get up and explain that she's got it all wrong, but because my parents think I'm sleeping, I don't dare; I squeeze my eyes shut instead and suddenly I'm in a world

where

there are many of me.

One for Grandma during the long, gray winter days, a girl who knows how to wash dishes and has blonde hair and makes macaroni casserole before Grandpa comes home from work.

One for Grandpa, a girl who is brave enough not to go to school since it's the pointless, silly province of the rich.

One for Mother, a girl who's energetic and likes sports and wearing skirts and who participates in the Finnish Workers' Sports Federation's gymnastics' club and wins medals.

One for Father, a girl who's sure on her feet as soon as she puts on a pair of hockey skates and who can ride a bike faster and more confidently than any boy.

And one who's a boy, and that's me.

He spits and goes wherever he wants and doesn't care about anybody or anything.

Inevitably the day arrives when Grandma and Mother pack my things, and Father lifts the bags into the BMW's trunk.

I climb into the back seat without looking at anyone, but Mother makes me come back out into the yard.

"Now you tell Grandma and Grandpa, 'Thank you for the summer.'"

"Thank you for the summer," I say, staring at the ground.

Grandma stares over the spruce hedge and doesn't say a thing.

Grandpa is too busy to say anything either; he's pretending to fix the swing and jostles the supporting poles in feigned concentration.

"Damn thing's rotten through."

But Mother doesn't give up.

"Now say goodbye to Tepsi, too," Mother says.

"Bye, Tepsi," I say, not even looking in her direction.
Finally I'm allowed to get back in the car.
As Father drives through the gate onto the road, Mother
tells me to wave at Grandma and Grandpa and Tepsi.
I wave without turning my head.
I don't know if Grandma or Grandpa or Tepsi wave
back, but my guess is they don't.

We drive past the hawthorn hedge.
The swallows are there, chattering spitefully.
"All right," Father says. "Time to switch gears now."
Mother tries to poke him into silence with her elbow,
but he doesn't notice.
"We're gonna get some order and discipline back in
your life," Father goes on.
"Would you stop that," Mother whispers quietly, hop-
ing I won't hear. "She's sad enough as it is."
Mother's voice trembles with compassion,
and

she's furious at her mother for preventing her from
being strong and carefree and indifferent and a boy.

"Isn't Elsa with you?"

Father lifts his head from the depths of his pillow and tries to look past me.

"She'll be here soon," I say, taking his hand.

He pulls his hand away.

My idle hand seeks out a pocket, finds a lighter, and lingers there, stroking the warm metal surface.

"I need a cigarette," Father says, stubbornly staring into the empty hallway.

"They won't give you any," I say. "Apparently you've got fluid in your lungs."

"Everyone else smokes."

There's a little boy's defiance in Father's voice, and

she momentarily feels the petty desire to get back at her father for all of her childhood's meaningless rules and humiliating justifications:

"Why can't I?"

"You just can't."

"But why not?"

"Because I said no, and no means no."

But then Elsa arrives.

Her metal crutches click down the corridor.
Lost in the curtain folds, the sun throws a lone ray of light onto the metal, which flashes under Elsa's arm, and

she's forced to swallow her emotion as she looks at her glittering, black-haired daughter.
Even the old man forgets his IV drip and cranes his neck to see.
"It's Elsa."

"What happened to your leg?" Father asks, grabbing Elsa's hand.
Elsa holds my father's hand.
Tears quickly spring to Elsa's black-lashed eyes, but she smiles and strokes Father's cheek with her free hand.
"She had a corn removed," I answer on her behalf. "I told you that."
Father stares fixedly at Elsa.
"You get them from dancing too much," I say.
Father stares at Elsa and wrinkles his brow as if he's working hard to remember something. And Elsa lets the tears flow freely down her cheeks as she smiles her gentle, comforting smile at Father, who continues staring fixedly at her, my daughter, the one who gets to hold Father's hand, and

she's so overwhelmed by her irrevocable exclusion it takes her breath away.

Luckily just then a nurse walks by carrying a bottle of juice.

"Do you know how he's doing?" I ask.

The nurse stops and smiles.

She smiles at me.

I'd like to come up with something to say, something that would get the nurse to stay and talk to me, smile at me.

"He's pretty stable as far as I know," the nurse says and takes a few steps back, still holding the juice. "He's getting better, I'd say, but you can call for the doctor after his rounds in the morning…"

Then the nurse leaves and I'm all alone again, not sure where to put my idle hands.

"What does one of those rolls of movie film cost these days?" Father suddenly asks, his hand still in Elsa's.

"Hmm…an 8mm roll?" I ask, delighted by the sudden attention.

"Yeah."

"Seventy marks," I guess, as I expect Father won't ever be buying one again.

"I see," he says matter-of-factly. "Back in the day it cost thirty marks."

"I see," I respond just as matter-of-factly, thinking of Father back in the day, in a time that no longer exists.

But Father turns back to Elsa, furrowing his brow as

if trying to capture something, to remember the thing he's lost; he smiles and carefully extracts his hand from Elsa's.

His shaking finger wavers in the air, finds Elsa's nose.

"Boo," Father says tenderly.

"Boo," Elsa answers back, wiping her eyes and her cheeks on her sleeve.

"I always did that when you were little," Father whispers.

But you never did it to me! she cries out in her mind, and she's ashamed of the petty thought in the face of this fleeting tenderness.

She's ashamed of her dizzying jealousy and the submissive admiration she feels for her daughter's natural feminine affection and tenderness.

And

just now she doesn't want to remember the afternoon she and Father spent sitting behind the door that separated them from her mother who was recovering from a heart attack in the intensive care unit at Meilahti Hospital.

Father was a somber, handsome, middle-aged man then, and he stared at his hands balled into fists and got upset with her for crying.

"This is no place to blubber."

Well I will, she'd wanted to say.

But she didn't say anything; she simply got up, stifled her tears, and began rhythmically beating her head against the window pane behind which ambulances came and went.

The door finally opened, and a nurse stepped out into the hallway.

"Are you Alli Helena Mellberg's family?"

"Yes," Father answered. "She's our wife."

Elsa looks at me questioningly, her hand still in Father's.

"Well then," I say.

"So," Father says.

"I guess it's about time for me and Elsa to go."

Father's fingers tighten around Elsa's hand.

"Elsa, go get my clothes."

Elsa glances at me in alarm, and I look around for support, but there isn't a single nurse anywhere.

We're in a desert of old, sick men.

"You have a car," Father whispers eagerly, reaching toward me. "You could take me and Elsa somewhere nice where we can sit together."

I laugh, and Elsa laughs too, uneasily.

"I think you'll only need to stay here a few more nights," I lie.

Father presses his head back into the pillow.

"I see."

"Yeah," I say.

And then there's nothing left to do but to squeeze the hand that doesn't want to be squeezed.

"Try to hang in there."

"Got to," Father says into the pillow, and

we're at home.

My legs hurt.

I open the bottle of Calvados, and the smoke and apple flavors burn my tongue, when suddenly the phone rings.
"Let's not answer."
"We've got to," Elsa says.
"No we don't," I say, and

she still feels the sharp jab of Father's elbow in her side as they race to wash their hands and reach Mother, lying in bed and attached to various tubes.

They put on white coats and white gloves and a white mask with strings she doesn't bother to tie when she notices Father stuff his own mask in the pocket of his white coat.

But she catches up to Father before they reach the bed, and they stand on either side of Mother, out of breath.

Mother lies on the bed, white and translucent.

And she realizes Mother doesn't dare open her eyes because she isn't sure which jealous person she will see first.

"It's the hospital."
Elsa stands in the doorway; the light behind her makes her black hair glow white.
I slowly swallow the taste of smoke.
I walk in slow motion past a sleeping Aleksei, purring on his back on the sofa; past the bathroom where the light's been left on; past the kitchen's yellowed, peeling doorframe, which I now notice needs a coat of paint.
The receiver is next to the coffee machine.
I have to pick it up.

It feels cool and distant, but I have to lift it to my ear.

Father has died.

I can tell from the nurse's voice that this is a solemn, remarkable occasion.
"Aha," I hear myself say, even though in reality I'm looking out the window into the courtyard, only partially swallowed by the September darkness.
A resilient flower spreads its white veil over its wooden garden box, and I'm surprised I don't remember ever having seen it before.
And

all that's left is the journey past the peeling doorframe, past the needlessly lit bathroom, past the purring cat to Elsa standing on the rug with a questioning look in her eyes.
"Grandpa has died."
Elsa smiles momentarily before pressing herself against me.
I breathe into Elsa's hair, and my heart beats against her forehead.
I don't ever want to give up this pose, this moment with my daughter, and

I never did.

the zeppelin

I've seen zeppelins twice in my life.

The first time it was August.
At the end of July I'd left the maternity hospital, carrying a small bundle that was to become my daughter in one hand and a flaming red gladiolus as tall as a sword in the other.
The gladiolus refused to droop. Even in August, after I'd been abandoned, I sat on the sofa with an unfamiliar and mysterious child on my lap, staring at that conceited sword that refused to fall.
And then a zeppelin appeared in the window above the sword's tip, *Goodyear* splayed across its side. It floated across my field of vision like a nightmare in slow motion. It wished me a good year, and I couldn't believe it was real.

Now it's the first hot day of summer.
The deep, black pond is covered in a thin crust of ice.

I'm just about to break it when a silent zeppelin appears in the violet-blue sky.

The zeppelin hangs low, so low I could touch it with my hand.

Then it plunges over my head into the pond, and I open my mouth to scream for help but no sound escapes.

The zeppelin lies in the pond, and its gray, metallic roof sticks out of the water like the back of a great burbot.

I wade over to it.

Get up on the roof and find the ceiling hatch.

Open it.

And then the others come.

People walk over me, laughing and chattering.

They have picnic baskets with them.

There could be dead people in there, I try to say, but I'm the only one who has no voice at all.

I enter the zeppelin with the picknickers.

Inside, the zeppelin opens up into a huge palace.

The entrance hall is still lit, but because it's sinking, electricity has been cut from the rooms cordoned off by heavy salmon-red curtains.

The picknickers open their baskets and wine bottles, and with a sandwich or wineglass in hand, they start to empty the zeppelin like swarming termites.

You can't steal from the dead, I want to say, but now I can't even open my mouth.

The termites' feverish frenzy spreads to me.

I push my way through the crowd into a room where the silhouettes of lamps are visible in the gloom.

Lamp stands, lamp shades, crystal chandeliers—there are hundreds, no, thousands of them.

I'm the only one interested in the lamps, I can take them all.

But when I grab a lamp shade, it tears, and its bronze-cast stand crumbles to dust.

One crystal chandelier is made of fish scales.

Fortunately there are other rooms.

There's a hall filled with antique ornaments: garden gnomes with plump cheeks; a shepherd carved out of ebony playing a pan flute; twenty *Rebecca at the Well* reproductions; an odd pair of glazed earthenware twins sitting on a potty, one black and the other pink.

I light a candle that has appeared in my hand.

The gnome isn't three-dimensional after all, but flat and fashioned out of rusted sheetmetal.

The Rebeccas are flesh and blood but already in a state of decay.

Still, I refuse to give up.

In a glowing white hall I find a cabinet that covers the wall, full of small drawers.

I open the topmost drawer, and at the same time a cane with a curved handle pokes up from between my feet and opens the lowermost drawer.

Both drawers are empty.

All of them are empty.

I climb back out onto the zeppelin's roof.
Fall has arrived. The trees are engulfed in flames the color of blood, but the air smells like the cold of winter, like a clear, starlit night.

When I wake up, I remember that Father has died.
I decide to write this book.

immortality

Grandma and Aunt Hilma take me to the park to play. It's cloudy but dry, and behind the stone wall, cars grind their brakes and release thick smoke smelling of gasoline into the air.

It's cool and dark in the park.

The birches sigh wistfully on this late summer day.

A squirrel with a bushy tail stops to look at me with its glittering eyes before hopping daintily onto a rock and then onto the sturdy trunk of a pine tree.

There are quite a few rocks in the park.

They're shiny and smooth down the sides, and they're great for climbing.

The park is filled with flowers, too.

I gather a bouquet each for Grandma and Aunt Hilma: red flowers with tender stems whose name I don't know, and flimsy blue fluffballs that fall apart in my hands.

"Good Lord! Where did you get those?" Grandma asks.

"You're not supposed to pick the flowers here, dear child," Aunt Hilma says.

And Grandma explains that there are people lying

under the rocks, and all the flowers in the park belong to them.

As a teenager she grew to love cemeteries: the silence, the faintly rustling trees, the leisurely footfalls on gravel. She studied the names and numbers carved into the gravestones. The numbers cut a piece out of eternity, a period of time that had belonged to a single person and accommodated one birth, followed by so much haste and hassle; so many hopes, disappointments, and doubts—and one death.

She went to the cemetery in secret and alone; she walked between the gravestones, mumbling names and years out loud. She lost all sense of time and returned home calm and serene, somewhat dignified.

I no longer want to climb on the rocks; I sit down between Grandma and Aunt Hilma on a park bench and eat a sandwich.

Grandma and Aunt Hilma patiently explain the stages of life: first you live and do important things like chase fame and fortune, and then you die and end up in a white dress known as a burial gown that has no pockets at all.

"You can't take anything with you when it's time to go," Aunt Hilma says with gloomy satisfaction, and a melancholy but vindictive smile steals across Grandma's lips, too.

"Not one thing, so remember that."

The dead person in the white dress is put in a box called a coffin, the coffin is lowered deep into the ground, and a marble gravestone is put on top.

"It could also be made of granite," Aunt Hilma says.

"But it's usually made of marble," Grandma rebuts her.

And Aunt Hilma:

"They used to be marble. Now it's mostly granite."

And Grandma:

"Crosses used to be carved out of wood."

And Aunt Hilma:

"Crosses were made of marble back then, too. Just like now."

Aunt Ulla gives her a copy of *Spoon River Anthology* for Christmas, and right after the holidays, she takes her notebook with her to Malmi Cemetery.

Despite her numb fingers, she takes notes on the headstone inscriptions until it gets dark.

The frosted birch trees dangle their branches over the slushy pathways until darkness swallows them.

Hungry and wet, she finds the cemetery gate.

The gate is locked.

Her legs buckle in terror.

The cemetery is black, and the gravestones swell against the distant backdrop of glimmering lights. The trees spitefully drip water into her collar.

She isn't afraid of the dead, or the dark, or even being alone.

She's afraid of the moment she'll have to open her mouth and squeeze out that one pathetic and ridiculous word: *Help.*

And then the dress and the coffin supposedly disappear, and I don't understand why the flowers belong to the dead since Grandma and Aunt Hilma, talking over each other, insist that there aren't any people under the gravestones anymore.

"So where have the dead people gone?" I ask.

The wind hums, a squirrel's claws scrabble on bark, and I don't get an answer.

"Where are they?" I repeat.

Aunt Hilma and Grandma glance at each other over the top of my head—I notice.

"Why don't you go see where that squirrel's gone," Grandma says.

And Aunt Hilma:

"See if it wants a bite of your sandwich."

I stay put.

"Where do the dead go?" I ask again.

Grandma fiddles with the two brass fishtails that form the clasp of her purse, and Aunt Hilma rubs her sore foot.

"Well now," Aunt Hilma says carefully. "If only some-one knew for sure."

"Good people join God in heaven," Grandma says, glancing at Aunt Hilma out of the corner of her eye.

Aunt Hilma yawns,

and

she suddenly realizes Grandma and Aunt Hilma dis-agree about what happens to people after they die, and they don't want her to notice.

She realizes there isn't anyone who can speak defini-tively about death.

"There's clouds up there," Aunt Hilma says, not looking at me or at Grandma, who seems to be focused on watching the squirrel rather than me. "And then there's this ungodly amount of empty space, and then the stars."

"Those places haven't been explored yet," Grandma says mysteriously. "The space beyond the stars and all that."

"And that's where heaven is?" I ask.

"And you'd fall through the clouds with a whoosh," Aunt Hilma says. "If you tried to go stand up there."

"Why?" I ask.

"Unless you're a spirit," Grandma says. "If you're flesh and bones and still alive, I bet you would fall."

"You sure would," I say, because I guess that's what Grandpa's response would be.

"There are so many things…we don't understand," Grandma says.

"Yeah, like God's plans," I say.

"Scientists are always onto something new," Aunt Hilma says and gets up from the bench to straighten out her dress and move her leg that's fallen asleep. "Studies about the gases in the clouds and whatnot."

She never finishes writing her own *Spoon River Anthology*, but she doesn't give up visiting cemeteries.

There was the cemetery in Ilomantsi where she wandered around the moss and needle-covered walkways as a young writer, briefcase in hand, trying to come up with what to say at her first-ever literary event.

She rested her head against an ancient, groaning fir tree, breathed in the crisp fall air; she closed her eyes, grew calm.

There was the cemetery in Lappeenranta with the rowan tree and its ripening berries and the bench underneath its branches.
She sat on that bench with her first love.
The heat was sluggish, and her jealousy was suffocating.
They had broken up two years earlier, but it was only now, as her first love told her she was pregnant, that she felt cut off from her for good.
And yet she bravely leafed through the almanac with her, looking for a name for the baby that was separating them.
(It was a girl, and she was given the name she and her first love found together in the almanac under that rowan tree.)

I offer the squirrel a piece of bread.
It comes closer. Its black eyes are shiny and I'm scared.
I throw the bread. It hits a gravestone and falls among a patch of the red flowers with tender stems.
I run to catch up to Grandma and Aunt Hilma who are slowly walking toward the cemetery gate,

the very gate that ten years later will hold her prisoner for an agonizing hour.

"Did you give the squirrel some bread?" Grandma asks.
"Yes."

"And did it take it?" Aunt Hilma asks.

"Yes," I say, looking straight ahead so I won't have to look Grandma or Aunt Hilma in the eyes.

"Isn't that something," Grandma says.

"Squirrels don't usually care for bread," Aunt Hilma agrees.

Grandma stops to wipe the sweat from her neck with a handkerchief, even as a brisk breeze causes the birches to tremble.

"Our journey will end here, too," Grandma says with satisfaction, letting her eyes scan over the sea of gravestones as if it were a spacious and luxurious new apartment.

"And pretty soon, too, I'd wager," Aunt Hilma says, equally satisfied.

There was the Opatija Cemetery in Croatia with the forest of white crosses tinged with blue in the moonlight. Laminated photographs of the deceased were mounted on the crosses, and there under the eyes of a housewife with frizzy hair she laid her head on the shoulder of her second love.

Her second love looked dreamily past her, humming some melody that came to mind and reminding her of her mother.

There was the necropolis of the rich in Buenos Aires: narrow, paved pathways lined with lavish marble mausoleums as far as the eye could see.

It was blazing hot, and she found a narrow strip of shade beneath an angel consumed by eternal grief.

A rat scampered across the lid of a marble coffin decorated with gold engravings and protected by bronze swords; it sniffed the remains of some flowers that had withered long ago, and slipped behind the coffin.

There was a cemetery in Ireland with Celtic crosses staring out to sea. The sea struck its white, foaming teeth into the cemetery's banks, swallowing the ground rock by rock and blade by blade, just as it had swallowed many of the deceased, their crosses searched for in vain. Chives grew wild between the graves, and the relatives of the deceased used nail scissors to snip them into their bags.

"Do you want to die?" I ask Aunt Hilma when we're on the bus.

I'm sitting on Grandma's lap. I'm cramped and uncomfortable because of Grandma's belly.

"Oh, dear child, we all have to leave this world sometime," Aunt Hilma says.

"Yeah, but do you want to die?"

"Now that's not something we ask people," Grandma intervenes as she tries to clasp her hands together on my lap.

"Well I do," I say, staring relentlessly at Aunt Hilma who grows pensive.

"That's all right, she can ask," Aunt Hilma says, chuckling. "And why wouldn't it be nice to live another hundred or two hundred years?"

"But then what?" I press, and Aunt Hilma blinks in surprise.

"What's that?"

"Well what happens after that?"

Aunt Hilma chuckles again and glances at Grandma.

Grandma watches the scenery go by through the window, despite Aunt Hilma's pleading look.

"What happens then," Aunt Hilma says finally. "Well, you kick the bucket. And they close the coffin lid."

Aunt Hilma turns to stare intently at the electricity and telephone poles flashing past the window.

But I don't give up:

"And what if you didn't die?"

Aunt Hilma doesn't answer.

"What if you lived…"

"To the end of time," Aunt Hilma finishes my thought, and

now she regrets her question.

Aunt Hilma has said it out loud, the thing she fears: the end of time.

She's overcome by an intense bout of nausea, a feeling so powerful she's forced to grab the rail on the seatback in front of her and squeeze it until her fingers turn white; she feels herself falling away from time and space into an abyss that has no contours because it is boundless.

She's learned to play this dangerous game at bedtime.

She's learned to ask: *What if there weren't anything at all?*

She's even learned to revise the sentence: *What happens when there's nothing?*

And

it's the same question Aunt Hilma has just carelessly thrown in the air: *What happens when time ends?*

She's already heard of the thing called space.
Space never ends.
But what's beyond it?
Nothing?
What does it mean that there's nothing?

She's already asked Mother (who was fixing a run in her pantyhose with nail polish and whistling "The Ballad of Olavinlinna Castle") if there's anything in the world that never ever ends.
"Everything comes to an end sometime," Mother answered absentmindedly.
"Even space?" she asked, and Mother, not bothering to lift her eyes from her pantyhose, didn't notice how tightly she was squeezing the edge of the table.
"Well, I guess space must end, too."

At night, when the sounds on the other side of the alcove curtain have faded, she focuses on visualizing the border where time and space end, and there's nothing beyond it, not even emptiness, and for a fraction of a second she's overcome by a feeling of falling so intense she clings to the side of her bed.
Afterward, her heart slamming against her ribcage and her hairline sweaty, she returns to this time and place relieved and spent.

"Mother told me time won't ever end," I lie to Aunt Hilma.

Aunt Hilma blinks and looks again to Grandma for support.

And surprisingly Grandma comes to her aid:

"A person's time ends, but God's never does."

I don't understand her answer, but it's clear from Grandma's tone of voice that I should keep my lack of understanding to myself.

"And I wouldn't make it another 200 years like this anyways," Aunt Hilma says amicably. "But if I could be like I was as a young girl, if my leg were better...well, why not..."

Since I doubt I can invent immortality, I decide that when I grow up I'll invent a drug that will make old people young again

because

she believes in powers she has yet to discover but that she's sure will burst forth any minute now: she will be able to make old people young again and turn disappointment into joy and poverty into riches.

Maybe the adults forming a loose, attentive wall around her are unwittingly watching her, hungry and expectant. Maybe she's an elf, entrusted with Grandfather Frost's bag of gifts: success for Father and Karhu Vodka for Grandpa; eternity for Grandma, gambling luck for Aunt Ulla, and a gymnast daughter for Mother; Sundays off for everyone who works Mondays; nimble feet for the infirm; and youth for those who don't have it in them to live another 200 years in their wrinkled human form.

The cemetery on Crete sits above the city, up on the mountainside.

I'm there with my daughter.

We take in the scent of stone pines, the quiet hum of voices, and the calm murmuring of the sea, which has no shoreline to bother it until Turkey.

We walk between the gravestones, eating apricots, and I tell my daughter about Freud and Jung; she listens with interest, having barely passed her own Oedipal stage.

The moon quickly disappears behind the clouds.

It's pitch dark, and I can't see in front of me.

"It sure got dark," I say. "How are we going to find our way back now?"

"It's not dark," I hear my daughter say.

Her voice is growing faint. I try to follow her and bang my hip against a gravestone.

"Wait!" I yell. "I can't see a thing."

"What game are you playing?" I hear my daughter say. "It's really not funny."

And in the sudden, humiliating darkness of middle age, I fumble toward my daughter, who after much persuasion agrees to take my hand and lead me, the Oedipus who has lost her self-assurance, down the mountain and into the light of the tourist-filled street.

And there's Hietaniemi Cemetery, where she goes to escape the afternoon noise on Mechelininkatu, when she's already a little old, a little tired of it all.

The graves here consist of installations complete with swords and Roman-style helmets carved out of marble; iron chains and huge headstones decorated with bronze reliefs; neatly combed sand and fresh flower arrangements, frequently replaced.

A hare sits inside one of the squares of sand bordered by a set of chains, and it glances at her distrustfully before leaving a few droppings on the monument of the venerable dead and hopping away.

An unassuming, black, knee-high headstone has been left among the droppings and the anemones, crammed between two large marble headstones. The black stone is engraved with fresh gold-plated lettering and reads: Wilhelm Maximilian Rosenbaum. 18 March 1871– 9 April 1873.

Little Wilhelm Maximilian, who only managed to carve out a two-year slice of eternity 115 years ago, can't be free or attain immortality because the conceited people who know nothing of his fears or his desires or his struggle with death keep him here, shackled in useless, golden chains.

marlborough is off to war, hey!

Mother doesn't come from anywhere.

Mother isn't interested in where people are from or who their relatives are:

"You can choose your friends but not your family."

Mother is interested in singing.

We sing together during the day, until Mother goes to work for Irja Markkanen.

Mother knows lots of songs from her time in the Finland–Soviet Union Society Performers.

The songs have strange names with incomprehensible words: "The Hills of Manchuria," "Harbor Nights," "Dark Moldovan Girl," "The Scent of Bird Cherry Blossoms," and "The Varsovian."

"I must leave behind my beloved city, the open sea is calling me," Mother sings as she looks out the window. This is the same song she and the members of her troupe sing when all the children are laid out crosswise on the bed so we'll fit: there's Malla Jerrman, Immi, and Jammu; Risto Forssell, Seppo Järvi, and Markku; and me, the lone only child.

Immi, Jammu, Markku, Risto, and I were all born within three weeks of each other, and so people often compare us.

I'm the slowest walker and the fastest talker.

Risto's and Markku's fathers think their sons are too wild, while my father thinks I'm too quiet.

"She could be a little livelier," Father says. "She'd get by better in life."

Olli Forssell and Topi Järvi would both like to have a quiet daughter, but they don't get one.

The Forssells will have another boy, a shy, premature baby they'll name Antti, followed by Pentti; and the Järvis will have Kimmo, who is so much younger than the rest of us that he's almost like an only child.

"The comrades' glasses are full, they think back on their friends," the adults sing.

And:

"The exploiters lash our backs, it's the White Army we must face, we will fight and win or die, we don't yet know our fate…"

And:

"Onward, onward, down the road of battles, we march shoulder to shoulder, brothers and sisters together…"

And:

"Through valleys and over mountains the fighters advanced to strike their enemy and crush the Ataman…"

And:

"One great vision unites us though remote be the lands of our birth, foes may threaten and smite us, still we live to bring peace on Earth."

Someone next door at the Heinänens bangs their fist on the wall, but the troupe members refuse to quiet down.

"Let's lower our voices," Mother suggests.

But Father doesn't want to lower his voice; besides, the Heinänens bought a turntable and play their only record, *The Bridge on the River Kwai*, night after night.

"The children need to sleep," Mother whispers.

But we aren't sleeping: we're listening. And enjoying every minute.

Then the adults sing more softly:

"Once a dark Moldovan girl smiled and whispered to me…join me by the shore…let's watch the sunrise together…"

And it's my mother who sings most beautifully of all.

I fall asleep to her deep, enchanting voice.

Mother sings better than me and is more beautiful than me.

I'll never be as beautiful as Mother; when I grow up, I'll look like Aunt Ulla, since we're both Aries.

"She'll never get married," Father says, pointing at me. "Just as bullheaded as her aunt. No one's ever gonna want her."

"Oh yes someone will," Mother says, lifting me on her lap. "Pirkko's gonna have lots of children and we'll become Grandma and Grandpa. Isn't that right?"

But

she's too blissfully happy to respond, snug against Mother's blouse and greedily taking in her smell: lilac and lily-of-the-valley mixing with her warmth and sweat and something else,
which

she will recognize only much later as the smell of a self-aware woman.

Mother is also interested in acting and was an extra at Vallila Workers' Theater before she sang in the troupe.
But she was let go because she could never say her lines without laughing.
Mother laughs a lot, even when telling the story of how Arvi Tuomi fired her from the theater for laughing so much.
Liisa Tuomi is Arvi Tuomi's daughter, and Mother is very interested in her.
Mother and I look at Liisa Tuomi's picture in the movie magazine *Elokuva-Aitta*, and it's true: Liisa Tuomi looks just like Mother with her dark, curly hair and beaming smile.
Mother knows how to sing and dance, just like Liisa Tuomi does, and Mother could play the role of Annie Oakley just as well as Liisa Tuomi did.
Mother knows all the theater families in Finland: the Jurkkas, Roines, Rinnes, and Palos.
And she also knows what *Elokuva-Aitta* and tabloids like *Seura* don't tell you: the terrible price of immersing yourself in a role.

Mother lifts me onto her lap and tells me about parties that start out innocently in bright dining halls, where people daintily sip wine and champagne from footed glasses, but may end up in underground bars with people drinking straight from the bottle and fighting and even worse things. Everyone starts off dancing and singing so gaily the curtains swing—but wives can get mixed up in the folds. Everything is fun at night, but more faces than one end up white as sheets by morning. You could end up like Rauli Tuomi, Liisa Tuomi's sister, who to Liisa's great sorrow shot and killed herself, either because she was too sensitive or because she was drunk.

Or maybe because she had just performed the role of a writer who died with the final words: I live!

As Mother tells me about Rauli Tuomi and members of other great theater families, she fervently presses me against her chest.

"Children must tell their mothers everything, absolutely everything—remember that," Mother whispers.

But then a moment later Mother puts me down on the floor; she hums a little and looks at me mischievously:

"Never tell another person everything. Always keep something to yourself, something of your own, something secret. Do you understand?"

"Yes," I answer,

and

maybe I do.

Mother can't keep secrets; she always gets so excited about everything.

She gets restless before my birthday.

"Grandma bought you an expensive present," Mother says before long, if I haven't asked anything.

"So what is it?" I ask.

And Mother laughs happily:

"You know I can't tell you. Grandma would be terribly upset."

I can't fall asleep that evening and have to ask Mother to come to the alcove.

"So what's the present Grandma got me?"

Mother laughs again and strokes my forehead.

"I'm not telling because I can't."

But just two days later, Mother uses her hands to show me how big the present is, and since I'm already in school and know how to read, she tells me the present's first and last letters: the first is a *d*, and the last is an *l*.

I immediately guess the present is a doll.

Mother is disappointed, and the hands that indicated an object the size of an average pike two days ago now measure its height from the floor: the doll is almost as tall as me, at least up to my chin.

I have two weeks to dream about the doll.

I see a mannequin wearing a sailor's suit in a store window on Aleksanterinkatu.

"Is it that big?" I whisper to Mother, so Father, who has joined us for our evening walk, won't hear me.

"Bigger," Mother whispers back.

"Is it a boy?"

"Oh, yes," Mother says carelessly.

The doll I receive for my tenth birthday is the size of an average pike.

But I'm old enough to know the doll must have been expensive.

I curtsy to Grandma and go to the bathroom to swallow the bitter pill stuck in my throat.

The doll isn't a boy or a girl. There's nothing between its legs.

Still, I give it a boy's name: Mikko.

Sipa, the building superintendent's daughter, has the same doll, and its name is Marianne.

Since Mother isn't a real actor, she doesn't get tangled in the curtains in underground bars at night, and she doesn't get mistaken for other people's wives either.

But Uncle Veikko, Mother's brother, was a real actor and had roles in operettas at Varkaus Theater before going to war and ending up a refrigeration technician.

That's why Uncle Veikko drinks heavily throughout the '50s, until he joins the Adventist Church and stops drinking.

I don't get to know my uncle and his children until well into the '50s, at which point I go to elementary school and they go to church.

Uncle Veikko is short with black hair just like Mother, and he's happy like her too, but in more of a nervous way.

Uncle Veikko can't stay put in his chair, always pacing back and forth between the table and the bookshelf, telling funny stories nonstop.

And Uncle Veikko's family and Aunt Ulla and Mother and I all laugh at him, because we know he's playing the leading role.

Father says Uncle Veikko's cheerfulness comes from the fact that he stopped drinking and smoking at the same time, a combination that would try anyone's nerves.

Father doesn't think anyone should run around a room sweating and laughing; people should sit in their chairs, just like everyone else, and talk about cars or politics.

The best thing Father can say about someone is that they are sensible.

Sensible types are always men.

"What a woman," he says of the women he wants me to grow up to be like.

They're temperamental women who have a way with words and don't care what anyone else says—except for Father.

They have a Ph.D. in economics or are mining engineers, or else they're singers or ice dancers like the women Father meets through the Finland–Soviet Union Society and who are the Soviet versions of the ideal woman.

But they don't make a fuss about their professions or immerse themselves in their roles to the degree that ordinary people can't understand them, like the drunks in Mother's theater families; no, they drink just like other people, take a glass when they're offered one, and accept people as people are.

Every Christmas, Mother, Aunt Ulla, and Uncle Veikko reminisce about their mother, who would have become my cousins' and my grandmother if she'd only lived long enough for all of us to be born.
She's always singing in their stories, and in such a gay and clear voice that no one in the Ahlström Factory's residential complex had ever heard such a voice before. And when she died, they said singing died with her.
If she wasn't singing, she was worked up about something, like someone's bad behavior or social injustices. Then she'd grab a switch or wave her red flag, and the children and everyone at Ahlström's knew it was no time for games.

My grandmother looks thin and serious in her photographs, and she's passed down her sharp nose and flaring nostrils to all her children and grandchildren.
So

the first thing she will notice about her newborn daughter, wrapped in shiny foil after the C-section, is her flared nostrils, sticking out white and sharp from a red, swollen face.

My grandmother was born Anna Maria Mamia, the daughter of a landowner from Kuolemajärvi in Karelia;

she lived as she liked, in the beginning, and then as best she could, and she paid a big price for it.

When she was seventeen, Anna Maria fell in love with an itinerant painter by the name of Lindström.

Lindström painted scenes of river rapids on the walls of community centers—he was a kind of fresco painter. Anna Maria's parents must not have been too keen on their daughter's intentions to marry, if they even knew about them, and one night (the moon was shining—it had to shine), Anna Maria and Lindström eloped.

They were married in Varkaus, and over the course of their short marriage, they had two children: Hilkka and Veikko. Lindström joined the Reds during the Finnish Civil War, fought, lost, and fled to Russia.

He was officially pronounced dead in 1982.

Uncle Veikko, who was over sixty years old at the time, visited Aunt Ulla on her death bed to tell her the news. Aunt Ulla lay exhausted in her bed at Meilahti Hospital, afraid of the pain that the slightest movement would inflict on her cancer-ridden body.

"Well, I'm an orphan now," Uncle Veikko said. He had started drinking again, and he playfully punched his fist into the foot of Aunt Ulla's bed.

"Stop shaking the bed," Aunt Ulla whispered, her lips dry. "Don't fuckin' shake the bed like that."

After Father's death, she found some official documents in a bast-fiber basket in the walk-in closet at Hämeentie. According to the documents, Anna Maria Mamia had been twenty-four when she married a laborer by the name of Lindström. Lindström himself had been nineteen.

So there's no way Anna Maria could have been seventeen when she fled Kuolemajärvi because Lindström would have just barely turned twelve,

But despite the facts,

she refuses to give up her image of the large-eyed, sharp-nosed seventeen-year-old girl who, on a moonlit night in August (while the ripe rye dozed under the seductive spell of a secure life), left her home and her parents and everything she knew to join the long gray line of women at the Ahlström Factory for the sake of unconditional love.

Anna Maria was a proud young woman—you can see it in the photographs and in her nose—and she didn't return home after her husband disappeared; she stayed in Varkaus and continued working at the paper factory. But even pride has its limits, limits dictated by poverty and the need to make ends meet.

Anna Maria had a visitor one night. (The moon didn't shine—it didn't dare shine on a night like that.)

The visitor was from Russia, and he told Anna Maria that Lindström had died of hunger in a prison camp.

And

she isn't sure who narrated this scene.

It could be she's made it up.

In any case, Anna Maria was now a widow, the widow of someone who was still officially alive.

But Anna Maria and her children were genuinely alive, and they needed things like oatmeal, wool socks, wood, discipline, and sauna soap, as well as the protection of a man.

Anna Maria found August Aleksander.

He was a widower and a log foreman, a man twenty years her senior, a good man who had given up on life,

you can see it in the photographs,

and Anna Maria settled in to live with August Aleksander Mellberg.

August Aleksander Mellberg is my mother's father.
I never met him.

August Aleksander, originally from Ostrobothnia, ended up in Savo as a child. A silent, strange, and broken child, he got lost among the puns and proverbs of the witty people there.

August Aleksander was the second of two boys born out of wedlock to a maid, and he was a single parent to three children when he and Anna Maria started living together in the room they rented from the Ahlström Factory.

All but the youngest of August Aleksander's children had flown the nest by the time Aunt Ulla and my mother Alli were born.

August Aleksander's youngest, a girl named Aino, died of miliary tuberculosis when Mother was three; at the funeral she stood by the open coffin, a chubby-cheeked toddler in combat boots.

Mother and Father sent her to Rantasalmi for her second cousin's confirmation party when she was fourteen. Her relatives, whom she didn't know, studied her with curiosity, and after she grew tired of staring at her feet, she lifted her head to look at them.
"That girl has August Aleksander's gaze."
And her relatives used a razor blade to pry a photograph out of an album to give to her as a keepsake; it shows a bald, gentle-looking man with his eyes on the camera, and his gaze

is so heavy and broken that she can't imagine seeing another like it until she does decades later in her own mirror.

I have two photographs of Hilkka, Anna Maria's oldest daughter, Mother's half-sister, in the photo album I inherited from Aunt Ulla.
Aunt Hilkka has a healthy complexion, a classically beautiful woman with black hair and a sharp nose. All the women in my family wanted to look like her.
Aunt Hilkka was a trapeze artist in a traveling circus in her youth.
That's what all the women in my family would have liked to do.

But in the Ahlström Factory's working-class circles, joining a traveling circus was considered so shameful that my grandmother Anna Maria had to walk all the way to the neighboring village after work to stop the mail truck and give the driver a letter addressed to her daughter.

The official documents in Father's closet reveal that Aunt Hilkka had a son by an unknown father during her years in the circus. His name was Juhani, and he died when he was a year and a half.
Hilkka moved to Turku with her son, which was an odd place for anyone from the family to live.
But she still refuses to give up the image of her grandmother flying down the road in Leppävirta, out of breath and nostrils flaring, to hand over her letter, which she's addressed to a trapeze artist and not to some unwed mother hiding in the unimaginative city of Turku.

What happened to Aunt Hilkka is ultimately what happens to hotheaded girls with sharp noses in this world.
Aunt Hilkka fell in love with a good-for-nothing; they married and had four children together before she died of miliary tuberculosis in the heyday of her youth.
(In her imagination, tuberculosis had poison-green wings and seductive, cherry-red lips. And of course it had nostrils flared as wide as they could go.)

She gave her own daughter the name Elsa, on a whim, and later wondered about her choice, since she didn't particularly like the name Elsa.

She initially thought she must have named her after the children's book writer Elsa Beskow, but then she remembered that she didn't like Beskow's stories at all— she thought they were boring and overly sentimental.

Then she thought she must have subconsciously named her after her dead brother Esa.

But

among the official documents in Father's closet she finds a note that's a single line long. It states that Aunt Hilkka had a baby girl in the '30s, and though she only lived for a single day, she was given a rushed baptism and named Elsa.

In the '50s, when Aunt Hilkka had been in her grave for over ten years and her three surviving children had been given up for adoption, a man claiming to be Aunt Ulla's former brother-in-law appeared at her door.

Aunt Ulla vaguely recognized him, and even though his clothes were tattered, he was charming and asked if he could stay with her for just one night.

At the time, Aunt Ulla lived in the attic of a one-family home in northern Helsinki, and she couldn't think of any reason not to help him.

Aunt Ulla was in bed, and her visitor on a mattress on the floor, when the police put out an alert over the radio for a prisoner who had escaped from Kakola Prison.

The name and description both matched Aunt Ulla's visitor,

and

she couldn't help pestering her imagination, wondering what the evening light, filled with June birdsong and the scent of bird cherry blossoms, must have been like in her aunt's attic room after she heard the alert on the radio.

Another relative showed up at our place in the '70s.
She was Mother's cousin, whose mother had been born in Kuolemajärvi, just like Mother's mother.
She rang the doorbell and pushed her way inside with her bouquet, memories, and mink coat.
Mother made coffee, offered her cream pastries from Eho Bakery, and obediently but indifferently recalled things she didn't remember and didn't want to remember.
The cousin left, after several hugs and promises to stay in touch, and Mother took off her apron, threw herself on the sofa, and lit her first cigarette of the evening.
"All that fawning. They should have been around when we needed them."

August Aleksander died of a heart attack in a loggers' cabin when Mother was seven years old.
Mother heard about it on her way home from school:
"Your father's up and died!"
She went home, and Anna Maria arrived shortly after the whistle at Ahlström Factory blew to mark the end of the workday.

Anna Maria confirmed what Mother had heard and made a soup out of dried blueberries, and that was all that was said on the matter.

Life went on until Anna Maria herself died from an unknown wasting disease five years later.

The Winter War had been going on for a month. The hospital in Varkaus was full of dead war heroes and others sentenced to the same fate, so no one had any time to investigate a factory worker's cause of death.

Anna Maria Lindström, maiden name Mamia, had two underage girls with the last name Mellberg, one son on the front lines, one daughter in the circus, two husbands in the grave, and a good number of relatives fighting in the Karelian Isthmus when she died, so naturally there wasn't anyone available to stand up for fifteen-year-old Ulla and twelve-year-old Alli when a representative from Ahlström Factory showed up on the night of their mother's funeral to terminate their rental agreement and confiscate their household effects (table, chairs, and a dresser) to cover their unpaid rent.

Mother's family disintegrates into a nutritious humus of smells, images, lights, and photographs, until one evening she unexpectedly encounters a red-haired man. It's the beginning of the '90s, and she's on a ferry to Stockholm, just like the man is.

She drowsily enjoys the food and wine in the dining area and gives the man a reserved smile when he hesitantly stops at her table.

She guesses the man is one of her readers and prepares

herself to exchange a few pleasantries and give her auto-
graph, if that's something he would like.
But the man tells her he's her cousin, Aunt Hilkka's son
who was put up for adoption,
and

they stare at each other in silence.
And space—oblivious to the misery and tears and death
throes, the blood bonds and genetic ancestry—hums
between them like a cosmic blue void; they have nothing to say to each other.

Mother's large, sprawling family breeds legends, quick
escapes, and disappearances; cruel moonlight and
traveling circuses; accidents and frescoes. So I'm not
at all surprised when Mother cuts a picture of Queen
Elizabeth out of *Apu* magazine and claims that the
Queen looks so much like Aunt Ulla that she must be
related to us in one way or another.
The picture travels from one hand to the next among
the coffee cups, sugar tongs, and marble cake.
Queen Elizabeth smiles from her balcony, her diadem
held firmly in place on her permed black hair.
Aunt Ulla initially looks at the picture in amusement,
but then she lifts it closer to her face. (Aunt Ulla didn't
yet wear glasses in the '50s.)
A little later, on her way to the bathroom, Aunt Ulla
furtively studies her own face in the entryway mirror.
And

a month later Aunt Ulla has amassed quite a collection of pictures of Queen Elizabeth.

The Queen consecrating a dam.

The Queen on horseback, accompanied by her good and handsome duke.

The Queen receiving the French president, a man with a big nose and a flat head.

The Queen under a fountain, playing with her chubby, bad-tempered daughter and her son with protruding ears and neatly combed hair.

The Queen saluting by lifting her hand to her head neatly wrapped in a scarf.

And

now the resemblance is clear as day: Aunt Ulla and Queen Elizabeth look just like twins, chips off the same block.

The family that the winds of history have blown from Karelia to Savo and Savo to Russia, and from Ostrobothnia to Savo and Savo to Turku and Uusimaa and Satakunta, could easily have spread one of its seeds as far as England, and maybe even farther.

Aunt Ulla suddenly remembers a song called "Marlborough's Going Off to War, Hey!"

She doesn't remember anything else about it, like whose war it was and when Marlborough left.

We make some proper, strong coffee and try to work out whether Finland might have fought against England at some point.

No one remembers,
and it will be another ten years before we get a copy of
Otava's Big Encyclopedia in which you can check those
little things that cause arguments.

But we do remember that Finland belonged to Sweden
hundreds of years ago, and that Sweden carelessly sent
Finnish boys to fight its wars, just like Sven Tuuva, who
was played by the actor Veikko Sinisalo.
And then a song called "The Åland War" pops into
Mother's head; it's a song she had to learn by heart in
elementary school:
The Åland War was dreadful
Hurrah, hurrah hurrah
When three hundred British ships
sailed to Finland's shores
Sunfa-ra, sunfa-ra, sunfa-ralla-lalla-la
Hurrah, hurrah, hurrah!
And

a pearl shines among all the hurrahs: the crystal-clear
refrain casts its light on history's hidden past, linking
Aunt Ulla, Mother, and me to the throne of England.

chasms

I eat a piece of pie made of wet, moist mud in the park. The sand grits in my teeth and stings my throat, so I don't feel like eating any more.

I don't feel like eating potatoes with sauce in the evening either. My stomach burns so badly that I want nothing more than to lie on the new Asko sofa bed that we bought when Father still received a salary from the Finland–Soviet Union Society.

I have a high fever that night, and the alcove is filled with strangers who scream and laugh and run around and around and around the room.

A little girl strikes the floor with the heel of her red shoe and screams above everyone else: "Attention! Attention! Attention!"

"Mother's here, Mother's here." The voice is faint but persistent.

And when I open my eyes, the little girl with the red shoes disappears, and I see my worried mother holding her hand to my forehead.

I try to keep my eyes open because I'm afraid of the girl with the red shoes.

I try to hold on to Mother, but the little girl with the red shoes puts a tea cozy on her head and drags me off by the hand.

A chasm opens between Mother and me, and Mother moves further and further and further away as the little girl twirls me around and around and around the room until

I open my mouth and vomit, right onto a pair of black pants.

Mother apologizes, and when I open my eyes this time, I see Dr. Tammilehto sitting on the edge of the bed.

His glasses are frightening, but his smile is friendly.

Mother apprehensively asks about medication and offers to make Dr. Tammilehto a strong cup of coffee.

Father isn't around, so I guess Mother is playing for time.

Father hasn't received a salary from the Finland–Soviet Union Society in half a year, and he must have gone out to visit the Koskipatos and Kalervos, the Lehtonens and Jerrmans, and maybe even as far as the Forssells to borrow some money.

I'm right: the door opens, and a breathless Father pays Dr. Tammilehto his fee.

I feel sorry for Father; we haven't been able to afford gas for the BMW in weeks, so he must have run across half the city.

Dr. Tammilehto pockets his money and says I'll have to be put in a ward at Lastenlinna, the children's hospital.

My second cousins' mother ended up in a ward, and Artturi would have ended up in one, too, if he hadn't shot himself dead. There's also a woman who was sent to a ward for embezzling money intended for a children's charity, and she even has a song about her: "Hang down your head, Mrs. Sauramo, you better hang down your head and cry."

I don't want to go to a ward, even though I have dark hair and I ate a piece of mud pie and knew it wasn't allowed.

But that's where I end up, behind bars.

The bars are cold and white, and the paint is peeling off. The bars surround my bed on all sides so I can't escape, not even to pee; I have to wait for a nurse to lift me up and put me on the potty, which is made of the same ice-cold, white enamel as the bars.

I languish there for three weeks.

I do get water, but no bread.

They call food "nutrition" here. It's clear and transparent like water, and it enters my stomach through my nose.

Before I ended up here, I never would have believed it was possible to eat through your nose.

Just like I didn't believe that tuberculosis could live in dirt

because

despite not being quite six years old, she was already a skeptic.

Her heart pounding, she put herself in grave danger with empirical tests meant to overturn most of the claims with which she'd been brought up:

If you make a face at an adult, even behind their back, your face will stay that way forever.

If you pretend to be blind, you'll go blind.

If you lie, your nose will grow (straight out).

If you kill a spider, you'll die shortly thereafter.

If you curse God, you'll die immediately.

If you lie, you won't be able to sleep.

If you have a bad conscience, you won't be able to sleep (which is true) because your pillow will turn hard as stone (not true).

If you laugh at the disabled, you'll become disabled yourself.

If you borrow someone's cane for fun, you'll need one yourself before long.

If you turn the other cheek, your attacker will stop and never hit you again as long as you keep your cheeks available.

If you swear, your tongue will become paralyzed.

If you gape at an old person, your mouth will stay that way for the rest of your life.

Mother visits me every day; Father, Grandma, Aunt Ulla, and Grandpa visit on Sundays.

Grandpa is angry—not at me, even though I did eat dirt and got abdominal tuberculosis as punishment, but at the doctors, who don't give me food even though I am hungry; and at my parents, who are on the doctors' side. And when the bell rings signaling the end of the visiting period, Grandpa leaves his cap at the foot of my bed, as if forgetting it there.

When everyone's in the BMW (which Grandma has bought gas for), Grandpa pretends to suddenly remember his cap and comes back to get it.

Back in my room, he slips his hand under my pillow.

"Now don't show these to anyone."

After he's put on his cap and closed the door behind him, I look under the pillow to find a bag of Fazer's candy mix and two Da Capo chocolate bars.

When I'm allowed home, I don't need to eat through my nose anymore; I can have coffee and French bread, and Mother, Father, and I have a serious talk.

Father starts off by saying that this is going to be a conversation between grown-ups.

And it's not about mud pies—that case is closed.

Father talks for a while about the strong bonds of friendship between the people of Finland and the Soviet Union.

It's a bitter pill for the Finnish bourgeoisie to swallow, which is why the Finnish government doesn't support the comradely activities of the Finland–Soviet Union Society, which in turn is why Father has not received a paycheck in over half a year, and so the decision's been made to have Mother go to work and to find child care for me and to sell the BMW, and isn't that the most hellish thing about this, huh?

But we'll get through this together, right?

After the BMW glides down Fleminginkatu to the intersection with Helsinginkatu for the last time, we go inside and make strong coffee.

We'd gotten Eho Bakery's cream pastries earlier that day, two for each of us.

Mother cuts her second pastry in half for Father and me, and then we discuss what a nuisance it is to have a car in the city.

There's the insurance payments and the gas expenses, the maintenance and the oil changes, and the constant fear that someone will pick the lock, open the dashboard, connect some wires, and drive off with it. That person has a record, of course, and they're plastered to top it all off, so they drive the car into a wall or a traffic sign, and the insurance company claims the car. Then before you know it, who's sitting behind the wheel but some insurance company hotshot while the poor car owner is obliged to walk everwhere with nothing in his pockets but the few measly pennies the insurer has bothered to throw his way.

There are the visits to the car wash, and all the people who borrow it, and when you get it back, something always sags where it shouldn't.

There are the flat tires and the broken windshield wipers and the jealous neighbors, who don't even have a driver's license, much less a car.

And the road maps are useless, too, so you always have to stop and ask where to turn and what to do next.

So it's really for the best if you don't own a car what with all the worry and grief it entails in this country today.

Especially when there are trains and buses and taxis that will take you anywhere you want to go, and you don't have to lift so much as a finger.

But

six months after Mother has started working a paying job, a well-used, black Volga gleams on Fleminginkatu, and it's just the beginning of the army of new Moskvitches and Ladas to come.

After all,

a person should have their own wheels if they want to go somewhere and take a film projector, their family, or some camping gear along with them.

And from that point on, we all go our separate ways in the morning, the three of us: Father goes to his office in Kaisaniemi, Mother goes to Markkanen's store across the street, and I go to Aili Honkanen's home down the street.

I immediately learn something new and important on that first day at Aili's, and it isn't nonsense at all, even though I initially think it is: if you stick your head under a downspout and let rainwater get in your collar, you'll get sick.

It triggers a high fever, and Mother stays home with me for three wonderful days.

Mother gets an advance from Irja Markkanen and makes cardamom buns.

I get to be Mother's biggest, most precious bun, and she covers me in a towel so I can rise. Only Mother doesn't shove me in the oven—she gobbles me up raw.

But then Mother disappears behind the store window again, and I stay with Aili until I'm offered a spot in a preschool in Vallila, where Aili picks me up in the afternoons.

The women at the preschool wear completely different clothes than Mother, Grandma, Aunt Ulla, and Aili Honkanen do.

She doesn't know the word for uniform yet, but the blue-checkered dresses and spotless white aprons fill her with the same horror that nurses' hats and Scout scarves do, and that track suits will later.

I don't like preschool, where women I don't know pat my head and maneuver me around, but I'm willing to comply for the sake of the friendship between the people of Finland and the Soviet Union.

For two weeks I go to preschool every morning, swallowing the pill that's rising in my throat. I go to the bathroom often because I'm so nervous my stomach hurts and I have constant diarrhea, which for the sake of the friendship between our countries I can't bring myself to mention to anyone, especially not to Mother, since she thinks it's fun to go to work and meet lots of people, just like in the old days when she used to work at the Vallila Workers' Theater and perform in the troupe.

But after two weeks the preschool teachers come up with a game called Spin the Silk Thread.

The game begins innocently enough, and I stumble around in the circle with the others, even though I don't know the words to the song and I need to go to the bathroom again.

Suddenly everyone stops and looks at me.

I'm asked to turn around with my back to the circle.

I don't want to turn around.

I'm told that everyone turns around when they're out and that, at the end of the game, there's only one person facing the right way around, and they're the winner.

I refuse to comply.

I'm told the game won't be any fun if someone refuses to follow the rules, and that in that sense, the game is just like real life.

I refuse.

Now I'm told we're playing the game in a preschool center owned by the city, and that there's a long line of children waiting outside the door who are eager to come in and play.

I refuse to budge.

The children begin to fidget in their wool socks and tasseled slippers, and their increasing restlessness is the teachers' signal to move from words to action: I'm lifted up in the air.

I smell underarm sweat and milk soup with noodles, and I struggle against my captor.

Another teacher comes to help, and now the sweat and soup are mixed with North State cigarettes and hair burned on a curling iron, accompanied by heavy breathing and the words *learning* and *only children* and *time-consuming cases*.

I'm forced to stand in the corner for the duration of playtime.

I swallow my rage and shame and tears.

And

the concrete wailing wall that's sprung up inside of her refuses to crumble without a firm decision: no one, not one single woman will ever touch her ever again.

On the way home I don't allow Aili to lift me over the train tracks.

Aili is puzzled, but she doesn't make the mistake of lifting me by force; instead she asks a man passing by to help.

The man puts his briefcase down and grips me under my arms to swing me over the tracks; he smiles and lifts his hat to Aili.

Still, I refuse to go anywhere where I might be forced to play Spin the Silk Thread again.

Aili stops by for evening coffee and apprehensively suggests that the trips to preschool could become long and difficult if she has to wait for the briefcase man to lift

me over the tracks every morning and afternoon.
Father is as furious as the preschool teachers in their starched aprons,
but

Mother takes the next day off.
We don't make cardamom buns this time; instead we stop by the Arena Building in Hakaniemi. It has a funny shape: if you follow the red brick wall, you'll end up exactly where you started after just three turns.
There's a movie theater in the building, but we aren't there to see *Pekka and Pätkä*, or *Alice in Wonderland*, or *Lady and the Tramp*.
We take the elevator to the fifth floor, ring the doorbell, and enter a room full of children. It smells like pee.
I'm relieved to get out of there,
but

the next morning, Mother dresses me before I'm even properly awake, and Father drags me along Fleming-inkatu, past Bear Park, and down Porthaninkatu to the Arena Building in the pitch dark of autumn; and by the time I feel another bout of diarrhea coming, Father is already gone, and the woman from the fifth floor smiles broadly at me as she takes off my mittens, coat, and scarf.
I'm allowed to keep on my felt boots and wool cardigan, because apparently the heating acts up.
"For now," the woman smiles.
I'm there all day.

We don't go outside at all because there aren't enough teachers, *for now*, and there are a lot of cars on the street. But that doesn't matter.

We don't have naptime either because there aren't any beds, *for now*, and as it so happens, there won't be any beds coming at all because there isn't enough floor space.

That doesn't matter, just like it doesn't matter that the staff here don't wear blue-checkered dresses or starched aprons—they wear pleated skirts and their own shirts.

It does matter a little that there's only one toilet, and I end up peeing my pants before it's my turn to go.

There aren't any spare clothes, so I wear my wet pants and socks for the rest of the day.

Mother refuses to send me there again,

so

she takes another day off.

We go to Hakaniemi, and we aren't in a hurry and my stomach doesn't hurt.

We stop by Hakaniemi Market Hall to buy Baltic herring and pickled beetroot.

It's dark and smells like meat inside the market, but I get to hold Mother's hand; the rutabagas and freshly dug-up carrots smell like a basement, which reminds me of Grandma and makes me suddenly miss her.

Mother also buys a loaf of braided cardamom bread, then we go visit Aunt Hilma and Aunt Helmi,

and

the next morning Aunt Hilma appears at our door before Mother and Father have left for work.

I don't have to get up, and my stomach doesn't hurt.

Aunt Hilma sits down on the edge of my bed with a coffee cup in hand.

"Sleep as long as you like."

I close my eyes, and I don't wake up until Aunt Hilma nudges me.

"Get up now and join me for coffee, so I don't have to sit here by myself all day."

Aunt Hilma and I drink coffee together, and she reads me the news from *Työkansan Sanomat*.

We play with my bear Kalevi and my sheep Ulla.

"Here comes the bear, grrr," Aunt Hilma says, yawning. I try to make Aunt Hilma understand that Kalevi is a very nice bear who doesn't growl at people or sheep.

"I see," Aunt Hilma says. "Why don't we take a nap, and then we'll make some strong coffee."

But just then I notice that it's snowed outside.

A blanket of feathery flakes covers the windowsills and the street, and the building superintendent's son from across the way has gotten out his sled.

The sled doesn't slide, but the boy pushes it forcefully down Fleminginkatu and laughs at his father who wipes flakes from his fur cap with a mitten and studies the dark clouds overhead.

"I'm going out!" I yell. "I want my sled!"

I don't get to use my sled because it's all the way down in the basement, but Aunt Hilma agrees to stand by the door to the courtyard, shivering with her cane, as I try

to catch the flakes floating around me with my tongue.
"Don't swallow them now!" Aunt Hilma yells. "Remember
what happened. With that dirt and all."
I don't swallow any snow and try to make a snowball
instead.
I manage to make one, but it's half dirt and dead grass.
I throw the ball against the wall.
"Don't you throw any snowballs at a window!" Aunt
Hilma yells.
I stop throwing snowballs.
I lie down on my back next to the rug racks, on a spot
where just yesterday there was nothing but dry grass;
now it's covered in a thin, even layer of snow.
I make a snow angel.
"That's no place to lie down!" Aunt Hilma yells. "You'll
get your clothes dirty. What's your mother gonna say?"
I get up and try to come up with something else to do.
"Let's go inside," Aunt Hilma yells. "Let's make some
coffee and take a little break."
And

a week later Mother notices I'm shy and pale, and that
six pounds of coffee have disappeared.
And

Mother takes a day off.
We go out early for a walk. The sun hasn't yet come up,
and we wave at Irja Markkanen who is unlocking the
padlock on her store.
She doesn't notice us, and Mother blushes.

We walk all the way to Kaisaniemi.

It's dark but crisp out. My nose is dry inside; it's below freezing, and my breath is foggy.

We visit Father at his office to warm up.

His office is full of the same kinds of canisters that he uses to store nails and screws on our bathroom shelves at home. But these canisters are full of rolls of film.

I'm allowed to hold one of the rolls up to the light. It's the same picture many times over. You have to let the film spool through your fingers for several yards before you notice the picture has changed slightly.

"Yes, every picture is different," Father explains. "It's just that the human eye can't detect it. Twenty-four frames pass through the projector in one second… Careful, don't get any fingerprints on that."

Mother and Father hug and nudge each other a little, while I stare out the window at the street turning white, until we're finally warm, Mother and I, and we head off to the Forssells for coffee.

And

on his way to work the next morning, Father takes me to the Forssells for the whole day.

The Forssells live in a basement apartment on the edge of Kaisaniemi Park. It's convenient because you can go in and out through the kitchen window.

The park grass sparkles and crunches underfoot. Risto and I share his sled, and no one orders us around, since Aunt Eeva has her hands full with Antti.

Antti was born prematurely, and the apartment is cold and damp, so Antti plays with his wooden horse while wrapped in a blanket.

The Forssells only have a few things and clear rules, but since no one has told me and Risto not to paint the kitchen window with a perch we've dipped in cream, Aunt Eeva can't really be angry about it, even though she frets over it with tears in her eyes.

When it snows, Aunt Eeva smiles and calls out from the kitchen that it's raining money again.

And Uncle Olli quickly gets out of bed and climbs up on people's rooftops to push off the snow.

Uncle Olli would rather work as a carpenter, but since he can't find that kind of work in winter, he gets up on the rooftops, even though he's so afraid of heights it makes him vomit—but only after work when he's back at home.

I get to go to the Forssells until spring, when I have my annual physical.

The doctor prescribes calcium for my bones and pre-school for my social development.

I'm taken to a preschool called Alppimaja.

"You better not cause any trouble now," Father says, and Mother:

"There'll be games and crafts and singing, and all kinds of things to do."

And

my stomach hurts again in the mornings.

Alppimaja smells of gruel, floor polish, pee, and fear, but I pretend to be calm as I take off my coat, mittens, scarf, boots, and hat and hang them on one of the hooks reserved for the Buttercups.

All day long I thread beads onto a string and play Sleeping Beauty; I draw the sky, the sun, flowers, clouds, and the Finnish flag with Porvoo-brand oil pastels; I eat potatoes in sauce (I put the onions in my cardigan pocket to give to Mother); I stretch like a cat arching its back and fly free like a butterfly past the stall bars, waiting for the afternoon when rich kids and only children are sent home and the poor children from big families are laid on folding cots to take naps.

My stomach stops hurting as soon as I'm on the street.

I look left and then right on Kaarlenkatu, and then left once more before I cross the street.

I stop at Markkanen's store, where Mother slips me a Ruusu chocolate bar or some licorice.

I look left and then right on Fleminginkatu, and then left once more.

And then I'm finally home.

A glass of milk and some bologna sandwiches wrapped in wax paper are waiting for me by the window next to the Bolinder refrigerator.

I eat and drink all alone and hope no one will ring the doorbell and ask me to be a cat or draw the Easter Bunny or say grace at the table.

The growing separation between her and her mother is creating thin cracks in her mind, and looking into them,

she can already sense their endless, dizzying depths.
But it's not until she goes to Alppimaja that she gets to know someone who will split the cracks into a gaping, insurmountable chasm.

There's someone at preschool whom I don't see at home or at the Forssells.
This person doesn't show themselves at preschool either, but they're there: behind the curtains or the door, in the air, under the lamp, or in the kitchen or the toybox.
This person's name is Jesus.

"You don't know Jesus?" Teacher Outi asks me on my first day. Based on her tone and the glance she exchanges with Teacher Kerttu, I understand that my very existence as a Buttercup is in danger.
The others at the table giggle at me. Only Niiranen doesn't giggle, but that's because the teachers have taped his mouth shut with a bandaid for spitting out his onions.
I try my best to remember, but I'm forced to admit I don't know anyone by that name.

I'm told Jesus is the son of God, and an only child, which of course cheers me up.
Grandma knows about God, but she's never mentioned anything about Jesus.
I share what I've learned about Jesus with Mother and Father as soon as they come in the door that evening.
"Umm-hmm," Mother says, pulling wool socks on her feet; our windows are so drafty in fall and winter that

even the curtain in the alcove flutters on its own.

Father doesn't say anything until he's finished his plate of cabbage casserole and lit a cigarette.

"There's never been anybody named Jesus. Scholars have proven it."

I share this with Teacher Outi and Teacher Kerttu the next morning, as soon as I've put on my slippers and stepped into the Buttercup room that smells of floor wax. Teacher Outi and Teacher Kerttu look at each other again, and red spots appear on Teacher Kerttu's cheeks. But Teacher Outi, with darker hair and a more assertive personality, wants to know who's said so and where it's been proven.

I relay this question to Father that evening, before he's had a chance to take off his coat.

Red spots appear on his cheeks.

"Scholars have known this for ages. But religion's always been used to oppress the people. Religion is the opium of the masses."

I don't know what *religion* and *opium* are, and I only have a vague understanding of what *the masses* means, but I try to memorize this answer.

"Don't tell her things like that," Mother says. "They may start discriminating against her and persecute her."

"What does *discriminate* mean?" I ask.

"We should have the guts to say things as they are," Father says to Mother.

"Yes, yes, but *discriminate*—what does it mean?" I ask

again. But Father has already opened the paper, and Mother has disappeared into the kitchenette.

The gas whooshes, a bag of potatoes rustles open.

"And what does *persecute* mean?" I try.

"Jesus was invented by the bourgeoisie," Father says.

And Mother:

"Turn on the radio. That Uncle Markus of yours should be coming on any second."

Teacher Kerttu shows me a picture of Jesus.

It's a puzzling picture.

Jesus has a beard like a man but a skirt and long hair like a woman.

Jesus isn't a man or a woman.

Jesus is interesting.

Jesus also has a lamb draped around their shoulders, and the lamb is arranged a little like Aunt Maija's fox with the glassy eyes that's called a stole.

Father, who shows pictures for a living, says that a picture is worth a thousand words, and so I tell Father I've seen a photo of Jesus as soon as I see him that evening.

Father laughs, and Mother does, too.

"But the camera wasn't even invented yet when Jesus was alive," Father says triumphantly.

I stare at Father, not understanding a thing.

"Or I mean when they say he was alive," Father quickly corrects himself.

So the picture doesn't prove anything after all.

I'm not sure this Jesus thing will ever be cleared up, even though Teacher Outi and especially Teacher Kerttu are excited by my sudden interest.

Jesus lived almost 2,000 years ago, which I'm told is a long time.

Jesus died and rose up from the grave, which normal people can't do, and started living again as an invisible presence.

Since Jesus is invisible, they can be in many places at once, and see and hear everything.

You can talk to Jesus out loud, and Jesus will reply—though not out loud.

Talking to Jesus is called praying.

The teachers talk to Jesus before and after we eat.

And at home you can—and should—talk to Jesus every night before bed.

I suggest to Mother that we talk to Jesus before I go into the alcove to sleep.

But I don't suggest it until one evening when Father is out at a meeting.

Surprisingly, Mother agrees.

We fold our hands and get down on our knees. (The second part is Mother's suggestion: we pray sitting down in preschool.)

"Now I lay me down to sleep, I pray the Lord my soul to keep. If I should die before I wake, I pray the Lord my soul to take," Mother says quickly, her eyes closed. Then she gets up and smooths out her skirt.

"All right then. Oh and amen."

I don't understand anything in the prayer, not what the Lord is or what a soul might be, but I don't want to ask Mother anything because I can tell she's embarrassed.

I start to feel embarrassed, too, first for asking Mother to do something that embarrasses her, and then for what I think embarrasses Mother most of all: the thought that Father could open the door in the middle of the prayer and find his wife crawling on the floor with her eyes closed.

I don't talk about Jesus to Mother anymore, because

she's been split in two.

It's a familiar feeling—it's happened to her before.

In fact she's been split into many selves: into one who's invisible and one who's present; into one who comforts and one who needs comforting; into one who's a girl and one who's a boy; into one who obeys and one who rebels.

Grandpa doesn't demand obedience.

Grandpa has never obeyed anyone, not even the Finnish government when he was called upon to chop steres of wood during the Continuation War.

"You started it, so you should be the ones to settle it," is what Grandpa said to the Finnish government.

Grandpa doesn't demand obedience from anyone, not even children or dogs—dogs should run around wild and free and smell whatever they like.

Grandpa doesn't want me to obey anyone either: I shouldn't come to the table when I'm called unless I'm hungry, and I definitely shouldn't go to school unless I feel like it.

But Grandma and Father demand obedience.

An obedient child immediately does what they're told, and never asks why.

Father would like me to ask less as it is, especially when Mother's out with her friends from her sewing circle and he wants to read the paper or listen to the quiz show on the radio in peace.

Mother would like me to be more athletic.

Mother has decided I'm going to be a gym teacher, since it's a respected profession that pays well, plus it's suitable for women and allows you to spend time outside.

Mother signs me up for the girls' gymnastics club run by the Finnish Workers' Sports Federation.

I have to go to practice every Wednesday evening, and my stomach starts hurting every Monday morning in anticipation.

Aunt Ulla is capricious, like me apparently, and wants random things from me.

She wants me to be a tomboy but to take better care of my nails.

Be invisible.
Be present.

Be present (for Grandpa). Be quiet (for Father).
Be invisible. Be quiet. Be present.
Be comforting (for Grandma).
Be energetic. Be beautiful. Be a tomboy (for Aunt Ulla).
Be energetic, quiet, present, and good company.
Be beautiful.
Be comforting. Be a tomboy.
Exist (for Mother).

But this is a new one: be aware of the invisible chasm
that has split open between Mother and Jesus.
And exist as if there is no chasm, hide it within herself.
Suffer for it.
Take pleasure in it.
Become an outsider.
Compare. Listen and watch. Judge.
Become an outsider.

Jesus is every child's best friend.
I'm a child, so Jesus is my best friend.
I stare intensely at pictures I now know are drawn or
painted: my happy, serene, and gentle long-haired
friend in a field among a large group of men in skirts;
my blue-eyed friend sitting on a rock surrounded by
children and mothers; my friend in a red skirt on a
mountain with a blue-tailed fish in one hand, a group of
people in headscarves at their feet; my friend in a park

with slicked-back hair, kneeling by a flat rock lit by a single ray of moonlight poking through a lonely cloud. And

she understands her new friend: lonely and despondent among so many people.

And her new friend understands her: despondent and lonely among so many people.

Since my new friend won't answer me out loud, I decide I don't need to talk out loud to them either.

And again I divide in two: into one who speaks meaningless words out loud—*Please bless our food, dear Jesus, amen* and *Thank you, Jesus, for this food, amen* (I don't think the monotony of the words interests my friend much at all)—and one who talks to my new friend about important, or trivial, things:

What if there isn't anything? Amen. What will happen when time ends? Amen. What comes after the end, what comes after the end? Amen, amen amen!

Or:

I can't sleep. Amen. I need to go pee. Amen. My knee hurts, amen, except now it doesn't hurt anymore, amen.

Or:

I simply let myself live in the shadow of a quiet, fragile presence. I clearly feel it; now I don't—now I do.

It's a ragged, hot, fleeting presence, and its unpredictable, capricious flickering turns her into a skeptic at a young age.

Those who lean into the shadows will fall into darkness.

Then the teachers throw me yet another curve ball.
They tell me my new friend can grant mercy; Jesus has that power too.
I don't understand a thing about mercy. I've never heard the word before.
And my teachers patiently explain that mercy is like forgiveness, but that it's somehow bigger than the regular kind of forgiveness.
I don't know this regular kind either—no one says they're sorry in my family.
"If someone hits you, you hit 'em right back." That's Father.
And Mother adds:
"But never start a fight yourself. Try talking first."

Being wrong, doing something wrong—it starts to excite her, because she comes to realize vaguely that transgressions are prerequisites to the blinding light of sudden and unpredictable redemption, and though she's never felt its presence, its contours are coming into focus.
Her gentle, capricious friend will abandon the hundred sheep obediently keeping to the path and run off after the sheep defiantly going astray because her new friend loves the sheep that's deliberately lost more than the hundred others.
Her teachers tell this story often, and she's puzzled by the contradiction her teachers don't seem to notice: Why are there so many rules, and why are the teachers

so strict about them, when breaking the rules is valued above following them?

One rainy morning Teacher Outi and Teacher Kerttu hand out watercolors, reminding us that watercolors usually aren't handed out to children until they're in elementary school and capable of handling them—uncoordinated hands can make a mess and splash paint everywhere: on clothes, tables, and the floor.

We agree to put only a small amount of water on our brushes at a time, swirl the brush just a few times in a single color, and not mix colors by ourselves.

I paint as I'm told: neatly, without splashing, using only a little water and only the colors provided in the tray.

The sky is a blue ribbon at the top of the page, the sun shines in the top corner, and the green grass at the bottom has a flower in the middle.

But Matti, or Niiranen as he's called, puts too much water on his brush; he splashes water and paint everywhere, and as a result, he's forced to stand in the corner for the rest of the hour.

Niiranen's painting is full of dirty gray swirls and flowers pulled up by their roots, and his sun glows a sickening green in the middle of the paper.

His painting is ugly and flouts the instructions, and even though he makes faces at us from the corner, Teacher Outi and Teacher Kerttu stand by his painting, heads together, whispering,

and

she's overcome by bitterness, though it's immature and therefore a paler green than Niiranen's sun.

Her teachers think Niiranen is interesting and not her. Her teachers act like her new friend, who tricks a hundred sheep into following them but still prefers the one that goes astray.

I want to be a lost sheep, but I don't dare.

I'd like to be Niiranen, who seems to be given countless opportunities for serious one-on-one conversations with the teachers.

The teachers smell of nail polish and perfume and look strict enough, but the truth is they're only interested in the Niiranens of the world, their smiles at the ready.

I've made the biggest mistake of my life by listening to Grandma and becoming a good girl.

The truth is I'm just a good, uninteresting girl, even though I have dark hair, and I'm an only child, and I have a Niiranen inside of me who wants to swear and spit out onions and break the rules so I can be punished with one-on-one conversations with my teachers and find my way into my friend's sudden, blinding light.

But

since she isn't the least bit interesting (she reads it in her teachers' approving, absent-minded smiles), she practices capturing the light of mercy on her own.

Luckily she has Kirsti.

Kirsti is also just a girl, but she isn't even an only child or a brunette.

Kirsti has two little brothers, and her father is a building superintendent on Helsinginkatu. She has a mother, too, but her mother doesn't say anything when her father buys skates for her brothers but not for her.

The truth is Kirsti doesn't care about skating, even though Kirsti borrows her skates when her own father isn't around to see.

The truth is Kirsti is interested in mercy and practicing it under the rose bushes during outdoor playtime.

First

I hit Kirsti on the cheek.

Kirsti turns to offer her other cheek, and even though it feels bad, I hit it with the same fist, which I've freed from my mitten.

Kirsti cries real tears if I accidentally hit her too hard and pretends to cry if I hit her gently the way I mean to. I fall to my knees and beg for forgiveness, and so long as the teachers don't blow the whistle right then and there, I can make tears flow down my cheeks, as I feel a strange, tingling thrill in my stomach.

Then it's Kirsti's turn.

Kirsti takes her hand out of her mitten, hits my cheek. I offer my other cheek, and Kirsti hits me again, and if I still don't feel it enough, I offer my first cheek again. And then we both cry, and Kirsti falls to her knees between the rose bushes, and the light of mercy is pale but burns powerfully in my stomach.

I watch Mother in the evenings.

Mother washes underwear in an enamel basin; she irons and mends my socks and hums; she smiles whenever she meets my black, hooded gaze.

Mother doesn't know anything about the hot, steamy springs that have welled up inside of me.

But

I give Mother one more chance.

My new friend shows up at preschool, and this time they aren't invisible at all: before me is a gentle man, bald and red-cheeked, wearing a black coat and unpolished shoes.

"I grant you mercy," my friend in the black coat says, handing each of us a black book with gold edges.

I'm sure he says plenty of other things, too, but I'm unable to remember them, even later. I'm too overwhelmed that my friend has agreed to become visible and serve as a bridge over the gaping chasm between Mother and me.

"Did he have a white collar?" Mother asks.

I try to remember.

"I think so," I say reluctantly because I have an inkling the collar will count against my new friend somehow.

"A minister!" Father says triumphantly. "So they're already running around our public preschools?"

And

the chasm remains.

narcissus' shadow

In early July 1998, the sun is most peculiar at five o'clock in the morning.

It rises behind the island from the northeast and paints the pine trees, the reeds, the tarred sauna, and a velvet duck gliding low over the water the color of newly clotted blood.

The gulls are screaming, of course, but from the island of Maantaustankartta she can also hear the deep cries of birds mating too late, a sound that she's incapable of translating into words.

A cargo ship chugs behind the island of Ruotsinluoto. The sound joins the roar of the open sea, which her ears can hardly capture anymore.

And her words are too blunt and worn out to draw even an indistinct picture of an imperfect auditory sensation.

She sits on the dock.

The water moves slightly beneath her feet: it's black and clear and red and incomprehensible.

The sauna glows red, too, but the tar is visible underneath, which isn't really black but rather a green darkened by

time, as something transparent grown opaque, like the glass in the sauna, which isn't really glass but an amorphous gelatin always in motion, restless, an opposing force to clarity, immobility, and permanence.
And

she shies from her words, those precise, razor-thin membranes that crumble at the edges, merging into the morning's prosodic muteness composed of sounds.
But

she still tries.
She descends into the cold, cloudy water and with her words tries to capture her image in the nasty, broken mirror.
But she doesn't see herself, the one no words can describe: the aimlessly swaying aquatic plants have stolen her image, too.
Even so

once she's out of the water she continues with the greatest lie: making words, building them out of weary characters, writing this book.

vitality

We have more than other people do.

We have a car and our Sunday walks; Lenin's *Collected Works* and Grandma's place; Mother's youth and communism; and Father's near teetotalism and the government child allowance, which we don't use for food or rent like other people on our street do—we use it to buy said child rain boots or a spring dress or hockey skates or whatever the child happens to need at any given time.

We're planning for the future: to buy property and move into our own apartment.

We save and make sure I get an education and fix things that are broken.

My parents no longer sleep on a mesh-frame bed; they sleep on a sofa bed.

And on Sundays we eat sailor's beef casserole and pork sirloin tied with extra sturdy string; we don't ever eat pea soup or Baltic herring fillets on Sundays.

We are moving up in the world, little by little.

We are moving up, the whole family is.

Father is the one moving us up.

Mother isn't opposed to it, but she always breaks into a doubtful hum whenever Father gets out a pen and graph paper notebook to plan things out.

Father gets Mother a sheepskin coat and me a tricycle from Bulgaria.

Tiitta's mother gets a sheepskin coat that's warmer and has straighter fur than Mother's coat, but Mother's still ashamed to run across the street to Markkanen's store in hers.

Father wheels the tricycle into the courtyard and watches me as he smokes an Armiro cigarette under the fire escape, just to make sure I don't lend my brand-new tricycle to anyone.

I ride between the trash cans and the clotheslines, and I sweat self-consciously because no one else has their own tricycle.

Everyone pretends they don't care, but before long two rows of staring eyes form between the clotheslines and the trash cans, and I'm forced to ride between them.

"Piece of crap," someone calls out from the first row, and the other row:

"A German one would be better."

Father doesn't hear or pretends not to hear.

"Go faster already," Father yells. "It can take it."

And I pedal and pedal until Father gets bored and goes inside and I can finally catch my breath.

"So did you let anybody use it?" Father asks me later when we're sitting down for evening coffee. He'd carried the tricycle inside to the doormat.

"No," I lie.

"You're lying," Father says in a frighteningly calm voice, and he doesn't cool down until I dig out everything I got for lending the tricycle from my pocket: five-mark bills, Buffalo Bill trading cards, and frayed angel stickers.

"Well I'll be damned," Father says happily. "Maybe this girl here has got some business sense after all."

But the Bulgarian tricycle, acquired through the Finland–Soviet Union Society, is just the beginning.

I get hockey skates, and Father takes me to the ice skating rink at Brahe Field.

My tight but comfortable felt boots are tugged off my feet, and I get hard shoes that squish my toes and have nasty blades glinting underneath.

I stumble across the rink holding Father's hand.

My ankles hurt, and I'm on my guard because I know Father will pull his hand away before long, just like he did when

the water was green and salty, and she had retreated into her own thoughts.

Her thoughts were clear and haphazard, just like the water, and Father's strong hand gently held her under her stomach, at the surface, until his hand suddenly disappeared and she fell into a surprising, burning darkness.

"Skating is great," Father says, and I stumble along, scared and trusting Father, who couldn't ever dream of having his own skates as a child until he'd worked for an old and irritable flower shop owner for a year.

I'm the only child on Fleminginkatu who has hockey skates, and I have no right to wish that someone would steal them.

The other children have attachable ice skates, if that.

They're the kind you screw to the bottoms of your shoes, ruining a perfectly good pair.

They have extra-wide blades so it's easy to stay upright—so easy, in fact, that you can't really call it ice skating.

But the hockey skates are just the beginning.

We get a movie camera.

People act completely differently on film than they do in a photograph.

People move on film.

Father mostly films Mother, but after Mother secretly whispers something to Father, he remembers to film me, too.

In one clip, I'm standing together with Tiitta, Airi, and Sipa, just like we would for a photograph, but then I take the initiative—because I know more about movie cameras than the other children do—and take a few steps forward.

Airi tries to inconspicuously pull me back by the sleeve, and her silly tug is as clear as day when Father develops the film and projects it on a sheet attached to the alcove's curtain with safety pins.

Now Airi can see the tug herself, and she blushes, but

Father and I laugh tolerantly and Mother offers juice and crumbled cookies that got damaged on the way to the store to all of us gathered to see a home movie projected on a sheet.

But even the movie camera is just the beginning.

We get a TV.

The TV is a box with the same kind of door our washing machine has.

But while our clothes spin behind the glass door of the washing machine, the TV's door shows films.

We also get the TV from the Finland–Soviet Union Society, and that's why it only shows Soviet programs, and the people speak Soviet.

We live on the second floor, but the TV antenna needs to be on the roof for us to get the clearest possible picture.

So Father rings the doorbells of all our neighbors above us, who have every right to refuse having an antenna cord pulled through their kitchenette windows.

But no one refuses because everyone wants to come over and watch TV.

And so Father climbs on the roof and screws in our shiny and uniquely shaped antenna. I wave at Father from the street and Father waves back at me, and I'm proud of my father who is constantly moving up and pulling Mother and me up with him.

But our apartment soon gets crowded; our neighbors ring the doorbell and come in to watch a scene in which it's snowing. You can make out people in heavy coats walking around speaking Russian and Estonian.

But even the TV is just the beginning.
Once everyone has gone home, Father is moving full steam ahead.
I'm ordered to go to bed, but I can hear Father's voice behind the alcove curtain.
He's talking about capital and surplus value:
When Mother sells Oka coffee, Jonathan apples, and Buffalo Bill chewing gum at Markkanen's store, the sales generate a surplus value that at present goes right into Irja Markkanen's pockets.
Mother objects and says Irja is a decent person who always pays her on time, and Father raises his voice.
This isn't about decency but about capitalism—Irja Markkanen is an exploiter and Mother is being exploited.
Mother is offended and walks off into the kitchenette.
Father swears to himself, then follows her.
The kitchenette is far enough away that I can't hear what Mother and Father say in there, but by the time I hear the chairs in the living room creak and the coffee cups clink amicably, the discussion has moved on to investments, loans, interest, and repayments.

Father buys Mother her own imported goods store.

But before she gives notice, Mother brings home a box filled with over 400 packs of Buffalo Bill chewing gum. I've collected twenty Buffalo Bill cards by lending out my Bulgarian tricycle, and I've gotten forty-nine more by trading duplicates and other things. But I'm still missing fifty-one unique cards.

Mother and I open every single pack of gum and buy the ones that I'm missing. Then we carefully rewrap the rest so no customer or Irja Markkanen will ever suspect that they've been opened.

Now I have an additional forty-eight cards and am only missing three.

Mother stealthily returns the box the next morning and brings home a new one in the evening.

We open 400 more packets of gum, but we don't find the three cards I'm missing.

And

that's when the inhumane greed at the heart of capitalism becomes clear to Mother and me: the last three cards don't exist.

Finnish children can go on chewing the stiff, vanilla-flavored chewing gum until their jaws are sorry, but there isn't anyone, not one single person, who will ever complete their card collection.

Mother's imported goods store is Finland's smallest grocery store,
since

the first kiosk to sell groceries won't open for another twenty years.

An article about Mother's store appears in *Työkansan Sanomat*.

Mother smiles in a beret next to a bunch of bananas and says she's always been interested in customer service.

The journalist also asked Father for his opinion:

"'Whether it's Finland's smallest or not,' a smiling Reino Saisio says, putting the last bags of coffee on a gleaming new shelf, 'your own store is still your own store.'"

Mother's store is on Viides Linja in Kallio's newly opened market hall, between Mantila's Butcher Shop and Eho Bakery.

Father has a rubber stamp made that reads: SAISIO Imported Goods.

In the evenings, after Mother has washed the dishes and Father has counted the day's earnings and sorted the different-sized coins into their respective plastic bags, we turn on the radio, stamp paper bags, and begin planning an expansion.

"My word," Mother says. "But we still have so much debt."

Father stops stamping bags and gets out his graph-lined notebook and his Finland–Soviet Union Society pen (which has replaced the messy copying pencil) and shows Mother just how much faster we could pay off our debts if we had a bigger store and Mother had additional help at her disposal, which would produce even more surplus value.

But Mother is hesitant to move too quickly because

she likes her store, the smallest grocery and imported goods store in Finland.

And I can run over to Viides Linja from Fleminginkatu to visit Mother, as long as I make sure my coat is buttoned properly, my hair is combed, and my face is relatively clean.

"What will customers think if the shopkeeper's child runs around looking like a gypsy?" Mother asks.

I'm not allowed to interrupt transactions either, no matter how important I think it is: I have to stop talking as soon as a customer approaches Mother and wait politely.

I stand to the side and watch Mother as she tends to a customer with a friendly smile.

"What can I get you?"

The customer asks for a pound of apples.

Mother picks the best apples, setting the bruised ones aside to take home later. She tucks the best apples in one of the paper bags I've stamped and then places the bag on the scale, which sinks slightly.

And Mother says:

"It's a little over a pound, is that all right?"

It's fine by the customer, so Mother writes the price on the side of the bag with the Finland–Soviet Union Society pen.

"Anything else today?"

The customer doesn't want any more Saisio imported goods, and Mother calculates the total in her head.

The customer amicably pays her, and Mother amicably gives them their change and sends them off with a goodbye that's tailored to each customer: it could be *You take care now* or *Here's to better weather*, or *Congratulations on your daughter's graduation*; or *Please send my regards to the hospital*; or *Your luck will turn, trust me—lightning never strikes the same place twice.*

I'm angry when the customer is a child, because Mother's time is wasted on them.

Children come up to the front and ask for a gummy bear. A gummy bear costs one mark, which is the smallest coin Finland bothers to make. Mother puts the gummy bear in one of the bags I've stamped, even though Father forbids it because the bag and the gummy bear add up to more than one mark.

Worst-case scenario, it's winter, and the money is tucked inside the child's mitten, which is in turn attached to their coat sleeve. Then Mother has to crawl out from behind the counter, undo the safety pin, and take the coin out of the mitten, then put the mitten back on and reattach the mitten to the sleeve with the safety pin.

That's when good customers end up waiting.

But Mother doesn't mind—she just opens the cash register, drops the mark in the till, and turns to her next customer with a smile.

"What can I get you?"

Father tries to give Mother pointers on customer service, but Mother pretends not to hear; she starts humming or changes the topic instead.

Father arrives after work during the store's busiest time of day; he goes down to the basement to pull on his brown grocer's coat and brings up Sirkku sugar, Suno detergent, and angry-tasting Georgian grapes (ordered via the Finland–Soviet Union Society); and he proceeds to set an example.

Smiling at a good customer, Father lowers his voice to ask:

"What's something tasty I can offer you today?"

And keeping his voice low, Father makes sure to recommend bananas to the good customer, since the fruit is just now at peak ripeness.

He shoos the children to the back of the line.

After closing time, Father carries the fruit back to the basement while Mother says *oh my* and wipes down the counter with a pair of underwear I've outgrown.

Good customers buy lots of fruit, only a few cigarettes, and no gummy bears at all.

Fruit has a good profit margin, but cigarettes don't. In the case of gummy bears, the profit margin disappears altogether what with the wasted paper bags and time.

The profit margin is what's left after Mother has paid all the bills.

Mother hums and whistles whenever Father talks about it. But even so

Mother's profit margin grows so big that Father's help during the busiest times is no longer enough, and

Mother is forced to take on outside help, which will produce more surplus value.

Father puts an ad in the paper: grocer's assisted wanted. Then there's a series of interviews, which Father conducts in our living room.

Our doorbell rings nonstop and interviewees end up waiting in line in the stairwell.

Father sits in the armchair with his pen and graph-ruled notebook in hand, and the interviewees sit on our Asko sofa bed.

Mother serves coffee and the donuts she's made the night before, even though Father thinks it's a waste. I rock back and forth on the chair in the kitchenette and watch Mother: after serving coffee she stares out the window and hides a yawn with her hand.

Father asks surprising questions and writes the answers in his notebook.

An overweight person won't do.

"They'd fill up the whole store," Father says after one such interviewee has closed the door behind them. "And constantly knock things off the shelves with their stomach."

We settle on Eila, who isn't too heavy or too thin or too quiet or too talkative.

After making our decision, we drink strong coffee and finish off the leftover donuts.

"So how's our new employer here?" Father asks, nudging Mother.

Mother wipes the sugar from her fingers on her apron and doesn't answer.

Father registers the store with Kesko Corporation, and Mother becomes a K grocery retailer.

But that's just the beginning.

After Kesko, Father signs up for a two-year correspondence course at the business institute.
And each evening after counting the day's earnings, Father orders Mother and me to be quiet.
Mother and I go out to Tuulensuu variety show theater to see short films and news reports or movies like *The Vagabond's Waltz* or *Pekka and Pätkä's Search for the Abominable Snowman*, but once we've seen them all, we go out for walks, just because.
We loop around Töölönlahti Bay and Hakaniemi Square; we walk slowly and take our time, talking about all sorts of things.
And I hope Father won't finish his studies for a very long time.
We stop to see Aunt Ulla, who's moved closer to us, to the workers' villas on Porvoonkatu.
But at Aunt Ulla's we have to talk in whispers because Reetta, Aunt Ulla's old, frail landlady, is sleeping by the tiled stove nearby.
When we return home, we find Father in a cloud of cigarette smoke, underlining something in his book.
"You should go to bed now, dear husband," Mother

says, boiling water for the dishes.

Father has dark circles under his eyes and can't quite comprehend what Mother is saying.

But

after Mother and I spend two winters in a row going on walks in the evenings, Father gets a class ring on his finger.

Aunt Ulla brings Father a round bottle, and he drinks the entire thing himself while Mother, Aunt Ulla, and I eat strawberry cake from Eho Bakery.

Father tells us about Dale Carnegie, who wrote a fine book called *How to Win Friends & Influence People*.

It includes the story of a kind man who always said good morning to the old, lonely woman he passed in the stairwell. He had no idea the woman was in fact very wealthy and childless, and after she died, she left her fortune to this friendly man who always wished her a good morning.

"You never know about people in this world," Father says in a slightly slurred voice. "You never can tell which tree the Devil is sitting in."

Then he starts to sing the folk song "One Rose Grows in the Valley."

Once he's finished the song, he vomits in the bathroom and passes out.

"He's earned it," Aunt Ulla says when she notices Mother and I are on the verge of tears.

Mother and Aunt Ulla carry Father to the sofa bed, and Aunt Ulla lifts me up next to Father.

"Go on and hold his hand now," Aunt Ulla says. "He's earned it."

I thrust my hand into Father's large one, and it disappears in its formidable warmth.

"…nice to everyone," Father mumbles under the blanket. "That's the key."

I don't know what to say. To my horror I notice that Father is crying.

But Father is his lively self again in the morning.

He's a certified salesman now.

Father has a diploma. There isn't anyone else on all of Fleminginkatu who has a diploma or their own store.

Father buys a briefcase.

It's made of pigskin, and it's the only briefcase on all of Fleminginkatu.

It's becoming clear that we need to move away from Fleminginkatu, and fast.

Father is lying on a bed in Maria Hospital's recovery room with his hair combed and a bouquet of pansies on his stomach.

But Father isn't recovering. He's dead.

One of Father's eyes is slightly open. I look into it, but it's not looking at me, or anything for that matter.

The room is tiled green, the air is cooler, and my mind is a complete blank.

I glance at my friend Kaija, whom I called to come view the body with Elsa and me.

She stares at the body, tears flowing from her compassionate, black-button eyes.

Elsa is crying too, but my eyes just wander from the tiles to the candle and its flame, which alternately shrinks and expands in the draft coming from the window.

A nurse pokes her head in the door.

"This is the only available space we had. I'm so sorry about that."

Aunt Ulla's body had been put in a cleaning supply closet at Meilahti Hospital.

The thoughtful nurses covered the mops and the vacuum with a green sheet.
Mother had been left in an operating room, growing colder amid the bright lights and instruments.

My hand is on Father's forehead, for the first time in my life.
"He's growing colder," I say,
and

suddenly she falls into the silent ellipsis of eternity, where there are no words, feelings, or time.
And she's still adrift deep inside herself when she leaves the body and presses her hand down on the metal handle of the hospital's front door.
A nurse calls out after her:
"This might seem inappropriate. But we have certain procedures to follow."
A paper is thrust toward her, and her hand appears not to shake as she signs it.
She's given a white plastic bag in exchange for the paper.

The bag contains the familiar glasses, dentures, and class ring.

the vision

I don't want to go to school.

Grandpa says children don't have to do anything they don't want to.

Grandpa knows plenty of people who didn't go to school and who've been quite successful in spite of it.

Grandpa gives himself as a prime example. He became a lathe operator and a homeowner without any schooling at all.

But the fever to move up in the world has spread to me too, so I agree to attend Aleksis Kivi Elementary School without setting any conditions.

To the very end I do hope I'll be allowed to wear shorts, which is what people are starting to call "summer pants," but with gritted teeth I pull on a yellow-checked skirt and a red-checked apron, because I'm told I can't serve my country without wearing an apron on the first day of September.

I decide I hate school, but after I get my first book, called *The ABC Book*, plus a pencil, a double-colored red and blue pencil, an eraser, and two graph-lined notebooks—all for free—I start to get excited about school, to Grandpa's and my own disappointment.

Besides, my teacher is young and dark-haired and smells like starch, and she knows how to explain the letters so they arrange themselves into words all by themselves.

The words line up neatly and take each other by the hand, and before Christmas I can read: Aaro likes apples. Antti drives a car.

Santa Claus, who has the same clairvoyant gifts God does, knows of my new ability and gives me a book for Christmas.

The name of the book is *Tiina*. It says so on the cover.

I can read the name by myself, and I read it out loud.

"Will you listen to that," Father says contentedly. "They've gotten something into that head of hers."

Grandpa pretends not to hear, but Aunt Ulla shows me another name that's printed on the cover.

And I read it out loud, too:

"Anni Polva."

"She reads effortlessly," Mother says, delighted.

I wonder aloud why the book has two names, and Aunt Ulla explains that Anni Polva is the person who wrote the book and she decided to call it *Tiina*.

I don't understand. Then I'm told Anni Polva made Tiina up, just as she made everything up that happens to Tiina. Anni Polva has come up with Tiina's mother and father and her school and everything else all in her own head.

Luckily, I've gotten other presents too—scented pens and chocolate, skis and poles, and a drunkard who pops out of a trashcan when you pull a lever—because I don't understand why I should read about someone named Tiina when she doesn't even really exist.

I don't understand what Anni Polva's imaginary world has to do with me.

I put the book in my toy chest under the bed and occasionally pull it out to look at the cover in the evening.

I've never read a book before.

And I've never seen anyone reading a book either.

We have lots of books.

More books than any other family on Fleminginkatu.

Two shelves filled solely with books.

The lighter yellow-brown books on the top shelf and the darker yellow-brown ones on the bottom shelf.

V.I. Lenin wrote the ones on the top shelf, and Joseph Stalin wrote the ones on the bottom shelf.

The books all have the same name: *Collected Works*.

But no one reads them.

Father reads the newspaper and does his homework, just like I do.

Mother reads *The Young Woman's Cookbook* in the kitchenette standing up.

The pages of the *Collected Works* form strange hoods because the pages haven't been separated, but Father doesn't seem to notice.

It's only

after three years of waiting impatiently to move that Father picks up the first part of V.I. Lenin's *Collected Works*, wipes the dust away with a dampened cloth cut from an old curtain, and throws the book in a Chiquita-branded crate.

But

to her disappointment, the books are restored to their pale auburn glory on the bookshelf in Puotila where the new living room still smells like wet paint and cement.

She's in secondary school by then and tired of hiding the works of Lenin and Stalin under her family's coats anytime her friends come to visit and then returning them to the bookshelf before Father comes home.

Mother understands the difficulty of her balancing act, seeing as there are forty-eight volumes of the *Collected Works* all told.

But it's another four years before she persuades Mother to help her carry all forty-eight volumes to the trash.

It's three o'clock in the morning, and the neighbors' windows have been dark for hours. Father is resting in Yalta on orders from the Soviet Union's Communist Party, but they still speak in whispers. The *Collected Works* are dumped into the trash bin, then Mother throws a week's worth of eggshells and fish guts and newspapers on top.

"No one will find them now," Mother whispers.

And she whispers back:

"Even if someone does, there's no way they'll know they're ours."

Then one day, probably in February, my teacher Aira Hokkanen who smells of chalk and starch sends me home early because I have a slight fever.

I play at home with Ulla, but it's hard to come up with anything to do with a stuffed sheep when you're alone in the city in winter.

I take out *Tiina*.

I look at the cover.

There's a picture of a girl my age. I'm certain the picture is of Tiina, who looks a little like me.

I smell the book.

It smells different than the *Collected Works* do: fresh and enticing somehow.

I open it.

I read the first line.

Since that goes pretty smoothly, I go on and read the next line.

I read the whole page.

I read the whole book.

And then

I lie on my bed and cry. I don't know why.

I don't know if I'm crying because the book ended too soon or because I read my first whole book.

Or because now I know I will go on to read many more books.

I close my eyes and see an endless desert of unread books before me; they form a pyramid, a vast sea, and there isn't a single volume of the *Collected Works* among them.

Or maybe I'm crying because I've been so blatantly lied to and told that Tiina doesn't really exist.

Tiina is more real than Sipa or Risto or Alf.

More real than Grandma and almost more real than Mother.

Tiina is more real than me.

But

suddenly the lights go out in her world, and her room and her bed sink into oblivion.

The windowpanes shatter to pieces. Screeching brakes interrupt her thoughts, the entire city sinks into a thrumming twilight, and she must push off from its bright, burning base to get back to the surface:

Why do certain people get to imagine little girls who don't really exist?

Who gets to, and why?

Who does?

Who?

Do I?

And

the question shakes her to her core because, though she's only seven, she's already learned to fear this unreliable, transient joy, the same one elicited by Jesus' secret, extravagant mercy and Miss Lunova's distant, dazzling love that promises the universe.

But despite her timid attempt at resistance, tearful joy rises from the deepest wellspring of her being, from the very pit of her stomach.

I'm still sobbing when Mother and Father come home from selling Saisio imported goods that evening.

Father stops on the threshold, passing his pigskin briefcase from one hand to the other.

"Jesus, what's wrong with her now?"

But I'm unfazed by the harsh words and the thermometer, the aspirin and the Ruusu chocolate bar because

mountains and valleys, sparkling winters and fickle springs open up before me; there are oceans and cities, screeching wails and sorrowful songs; clouds and processions; school days and the smell of asphalt; limping frogs and Stalin look-alikes with thick mustaches; ordinary mothers and brick rubble; African acrobats and coffee ads and evenings in the sauna; circuses, twins, and missing cigarette lighters; sadness, longing, the Miss Lunovas lost to the world; report cards, gravestones, and canned anchovies; tuberculosis and incomprehensible smells that dissipate in the wind; steamers sailing far away, the sweat in Mother's armpits; mournful tears

and fruit jellies; dirty dishpans and the secret passage-
ways of worms; regret for the little children who've died
for nothing and anticipation that smells like cinnamon.
And

everything that exists in the world is waiting for me to
capture it in books.

I leave the familiar glasses, dentures, and class ring on the floor in the entryway. They're inside an Alko plastic bag advertising the national alcohol monopoly; the hospital doesn't have bags stamped with its own logo.

"All right then," I say as I walk into the living room.

A useless moon rises behind Korkeasaari island. The wind has shifted and cuts across the surface of the water. Cool air finally streams in through the open window.

I sit down in the armchair. It feels different than it did two hours ago.

The table feels different, too. The newly risen moon licks the tabletop with its green light.

"Should we have some coffee?" Kaija asks delicately. "Or do you want some cognac?"

Aleksei has woken up and comes over to sniff gingerly at my pant leg, as if I now have the smell of an orphan. I am an orphan now.

"Cognac, please," I say, but then I remember. "I better not. It's a work day tomorrow."

"No way you're going to work tomorrow," Kaija says. "Not under any circumstances."

"No?"

Of course not.

I should call then.

I go into the kitchen and grab the receiver; it's warm again, warmer than it was two hours ago.

I remember that it's one o'clock in the morning.

I go back into the living room. My limbs throb from the need to do something.

"I think I might be a bit out of it." From Kaija's expression I can see that I am.

"Sit down and calm yourself," Kaija says. "Let's all sit here quietly for a moment."

Elsa and Kaija sit silently at the table, but I've been possessed by the green moon and keep pacing among the bookshelf, the entryway, and the kitchen.

The candles flicker in the cool draft, and the figures sitting at the table look like two granite boulders: one big, one small.

I grab the plastic bag with the dentures, glasses, and class ring.

And hear a faint cracking, as if I'm shattering inside.

I don't know where to put a dead person's dentures and glasses.

I sit down at the table and place the plastic bag in my lap, stroke it as if it were a cat.

The cracking continues, as I drink my cognac.

I drink another glass,

and

by early morning I've split in two.

The moon has exchanged its green light for a cold blue. And that color, so familiar and frightening and deceptive, calls to mind images buried in the sediment of my mind, images that have been hiding there for decades, absorbing gases and smells, words, colors, expressions—horror.

Cold eyes. Dismissive.

Demanding, threatening, mocking eyes.

Eyes whose blue-gray color turns black and cruel high above me, because I'm still little, so terribly small next to the one whose eyes challenge me endlessly to stand my ground, to obey, to fight.

"Nothing was ever good enough" escapes from my lips in a moan. "Nothing was ever enough, nothing, ever!"

That's the Complainer, dredging evidence from the sludge before Kaija's compassionate eyes in the wee hours of the night.

And the Tormentor is right behind the Complainer's shoulder:

"You're doing great—go on, go on!"

"Everything was wrong, always wrong," whines the Complainer, her voice rasping insecurely.

"That's it, keep at it!" mocks the Tormentor. "Classic, textbook case! The daughter of an overbearing father turns into a rebel, and nothing, not anything, is ever enough!"

"I always had to be something more, something else!" I hear the Complainer cry out.

And the Tormentor:

"That's it, keep going! Your father didn't accept you as

the girl you were, and then you went on to become a homosexual! Brilliant!"

And the Complainer:

"Nothing was ever good enough, never ever!"

And the Tormentor:

"That's it! Your controlling father despises your fanciful tendencies, so you become an artist prone to depression who hungrily and insatiably sweats blood and tears to buy your father's approval on every artistic front!"

When Kaija wakes me up, it's late morning and the room is blazing red.

She's tucked Elsa in on the sofa and cleared the table.

"Are you going to be all right if I go home to sleep?" Kaija whispers.

The door closes, and I stand on a blazing red battlefield weary and uncertain, as vulnerable and invulnerable as ever.

The Complainer and the Tormentor have fallen silent after their inconclusive battle, and I too am allowed to shed my armor and rest.

But

the sheets reject me, and I can't sleep.

And

now the sediment begins to thrust new images to the surface:

A little boy stands among bilberry bushes wearing a dress and a bow. He's forced to resemble his dead big sister; by himself he is nothing.

An eleven-year-old runs through the streets of a sleeting city to distribute the morning paper; he's sleepy, freezing cold, and confused. His father started to earn his living at the age of seven, and now his son can't understand that he's paying the price for this injustice.

A fifteen-year-old wins the regional track cycling championship and searches for his father in the stands in vain—his father never had anyone present to witness his own wrestling victories.

A seventeen-year-old silently endures a beating from his mother after an evening of dancing; she was forced to wed her husband-to-be after a humiliating pregnancy while he cast passionate and longing glances at her very own sister from the altar.

A thirty-five-year-old submits to weighing gummy bears in paper bags bearing his name after an exhausting evening of studying.

A fifty-one-year-old places the black-and-white high school graduation cap on his head and looks at himself in the mirror.

The cap is stored in a plastic bag and now belongs to her daughter, who has champagne cooling in the fridge for her own graduation party.

the secret

Now I have a secret.

It's a gate I can open whenever I want to escape.

Things are hazy and blue and certain behind the gate.

Behind the gate, there aren't any clocks, but there's time, and at the end of time, another gate opens that explains the end of time and cancels it out.

Behind the gate, I'm not a child but an adult.

Behind the gate, no one looks past me: everyone looks at me and sees me.

Behind the gate, I'm not in pieces but whole.

Behind the gate, I'm a writer.

I don't bother to tell anyone other than Mother about this writer business.

"Aha, I see," Mother says, mending one of my brown socks with blue thread since we don't have any brown thread. "That sounds nice."

Mother holds a darning mushroom, and her feet are

submerged in a bucket of hot water; her throat has been so scratchy all day that even her customers have commented on how hoarse she sounds.

"This didn't turn out anything special," Mother says, tying off the thread and cutting it with her teeth. "But no one's gonna see through your shoe."

No, you don't see, she thinks.
But you will.

For a moment I still wish Mother would ask me something about this writer business, but instead she gets up to boil water for evening coffee and whistles away in the kitchenette.

"Don't tell anyone about this," I try.

"About what now?"

"About what I told you."

"Yes, what was it you said?" I hear Mother's voice from behind the kitchenette's curtain,

and now

she wishes Mother would forget her confession, and she's disappointed when she realizes Mother has.

She's forced to open her secret gate more often than she would like because she isn't seen no matter how much she yearns to be.

She falls in love with Aira Hokkanen, her first teacher, who brims with starch, youth, and precise instructions, and wishes the object of her love would look at her even once with interest.

Then one day a miracle occurs: Aira Hokkanen asks to speak with her after the last class of the day.

With a pounding heart she waits as her classmates gather their things all too slowly, leaving the classroom an empty arena for the battle of desires between her and the teacher she adores.

Aira Hokkanen looks her in the eyes and smiles.

And she blushes in horror because at last she feels that she and her secret love will be seen.

But Aira Hokkanen only kindly remarks that she seems to be a nice and accommodating girl, and even though she smiles and mouths an *oh*, her hand is already opening the gate to escape the insult and disappointment.

She doesn't want to be nice and accommodating.

She wants to be difficult and interesting.

But she's in love and on alert, and so she remains waiting by the gate.

Her beloved suggests that going forward she sit next to someone else.

She's been sitting in the third row next to a sleepy, round-headed boy.

(The boy's name was Jouko, and he gladly gave her his things: his eraser, ruler, and Tunturi pastilles.)

Her beloved asks her to move to the fifth row and become deskmates with Kari, which Kari himself has requested. Kari had polio, which is why he limps and gets nervous and cries easily, and why everyone should consider Kari's needs and wishes.

And under the weight of her beloved's gaze, she agrees immediately, without setting any conditions,

and

with that careless decision, she seals her fate for decades:
To be cooperative. Accommodating.
To be mature for her age.
To be open and smiling.
To serve as a bridge between teachers and students, between leaders and their flocks.
To be interested. But uninteresting herself.
To look. But remain invisible.

Her beloved betrayed her three times, as is customary in great stories.

The first act of betrayal:
The next morning she obediently moves her things to her new desk and abandons a sleepy and stupefied Jouko who squints after her.

In the afternoon, the class plays Last Couple Out, and she ends up waiting for her limping deskmate, searching in vain for a knowing glance from her beloved to justify their defeat.

Her beloved glows with red cheeks and youth, and she laughs wildly as she hands out lollipops to the winners; her teacher has obviously forgotten her and their contract, which is founded on her maturity and should have at least guaranteed one discreet wink to seal the deal and acknowledge her sacrifice.

The second act of betrayal:

She kicks Kari's bad leg after he uses his elbow to jab her arm, which, to be sure, didn't have polio but does have sensitive skin.

Her beloved is roused from her desk by their girlish and uncontrolled tears, but instead of questioning them both, her beloved puts her in the corner, even though she was only defending herself.

She stands in the corner and tugs on her secret gate, but she can't get it open because her beloved goes on with the science lesson in a calm and ordinary voice, as if she hadn't betrayed anyone at all.

The third and worst act of betrayal:

Father buys her a pencil case with the multiplication tables printed on it for Christmas.

(Father was ahead of his time with this gift, too—pocket calculators weren't approved for use in math class until over twenty years later.)

She takes her pencil case to school in January, and she's proud of her pencil case, and her father, and herself for having that kind of pencil case and that kind of father.

She already knows the multiplication tables by heart and doesn't need the pencil case, but Father and her deskmate do.

When she and Kari get perfect scores on their math tests, her beloved becomes suspicious.

She proudly presents her Christmas present to her beloved, but her beloved's eyes turn black.

And by her beloved's almighty decree, their grades are lowered from a perfect ten to a frightening four.

Her deskmate cries as if his heart is broken, but she, the one who didn't have polio or permission to cry easily, and who is slow and stiff as it is, stares at her beloved with dry, empty eyes.

And her beloved relents and changes her deskmate's score to a seven, but she leaves her, the one who is mature, cooperative, and flexible, with the four.

On the way home she tears up her test, then yanks open her secret gate and steps into a world where she has permission to hate.

And to her surprise she notices how a love betrayed can fuel the flames of loathing, and just how juicy, profound, and pleasurable the feeling is.

I don't want to go to school anymore because hating Aira Hokkanen is exhausting.

For hours I've relished staring at Aira Hokkanen's face: her eyes are ugly and too close together, her nose is too narrow, and her smile is saccharine and phony.

I've looked for stains on Aira Hokkanen's blouse, blotches on her hands and face, and mistakes in her speech, and I've laughed spitefully at her blunders and slip-ups.

I've been filled with the power of my hatred, then

deflated again because Aira Hokkanen hasn't noticed a thing.

She gives me the same friendly, absent-minded smile she always has.

And now my hatred is mixed with guilt, which I try to quell by repeating Aira Hokkanen's three acts of betrayal over and over again in my mind.

But even hate loses steam, and I'm afraid of the moment when I will no longer be able to love or hate my teacher.

I'm afraid of

emptiness.

I'm afraid of feeling insignificant.

I'm afraid of becoming insignificant if I can't arouse Aira Hokkanen's love or fear.

That's why

I don't want to go to school.

But at eight years old, I know that going to school is compulsory in Finland, and that it applies to everyone, even children with polio, so it's either too late or too soon to refuse.

I decide to get sick.

It's not hard, since my stomach has been hurting every morning for years.

The burning pain morphs into cramps that cause me to curl up into a ball before school.

I hope Mother will order me to stay in bed all day, but she doesn't.

I'm forced to go to school doubled over in pain until

Mother can get an appointment for me at Lastenlinna.
The doctor doesn't find anything wrong with me, aside
from my constant anxiety, for which he prescribes exer-
cise and an early bedtime.
Because it's hard for me to fall asleep, I'm prescribed a
sedative, which Mother spoonfeeds me three evenings
in a row.
By the third evening Mother is fed up with my sighing and tossing and turning behind the curtain, so she
invites me to join her for evening coffee and throws the
medicine in the trash.

I go to school tired and irritated
until

November arrived.
The street was black and shiny, swollen behind the win-
dows wet with sleet.
I saw myself in the window: a chubby, bad-tempered
child.
I pulled on wool socks too tight for my feet.
A button was missing from my vest. Mother took a
five-mark bill out of her purse.
I stuffed it in my sock.

Then it came to me.

I wrote a sentence in my mind: *She didn't want to wake
up.*
I changed the sentence: *She didn't want to get up yet.*

I added another sentence to the first: *She was too tired to go to school.*
And then I improved the second sentence: *She was just too, too tired to go to school.*

I had become *she*, the one always under observation.
And

suddenly she was in a hurry to go to school to imprison Aira Hokkanen with her words.

Aira Hokkanen walks into the classroom and wishes everyone a good morning.
And she's unable to control her triumphant smile as she writes this sentence in her mind: *Aira Hokkanen was too, too tired to go to school because she had stayed up all night thinking about her terrible, very terrible deeds.*

dream words

I'm ten years old the first time I hear words in a dream. Images come first, of course, because dreams are made of images.

Everything's in black-and-white, just like the movies Father shows at Alppi Auditorium.

There's a car, and while I can't make out the make and model, it resembles a Volga or Pobeda.

It turns, tires squealing, in front of a stone apartment building.

And then comes the voice.

The voice says: *A large city, perhaps Moscow, long ago.*

Then I wake up.

It's morning. The light in the room is pale green, and gas hisses in the kitchen.

The boxes are ready and look like dark lumps from between the alcove curtains.

I want to fall asleep again. I want to hear the voice from the dream.

It's a man's voice, low and melodious.

I manage to glue the pieces of the dream back together. Two men in black coats jump out of the Pobeda. They run hunched over into the stone apartment building, carrying guns. Lightning strikes and splits open the street, and the voice returns: *Life in Moscow is dangerous.*

Words won't enter my dreams again for more than twenty years.

My dreams are filled with colors, distorted memories, and strange images fertilized with fear and longing, shattering well into the afternoon after I've woken up.

But when words return, they return for good.

And the voice that sprinkles words into my dreams is the same deep, warm, masculine voice from my Moscow dream. It hasn't aged along with me.

I'm twenty-seven and writing my first play when the voice, which has no physical form, suddenly says:

Put a band-aid on your wounds of love.

And the next night:

Use your hawk talons to pick up the sugar cubes one by one.

And the night after that:

Horses are slow birds.

And a week later, as my play is slipping through my fingers:

Quickly gather the pearls from the edge of your dream into your basket—they're melting.

Then the voice disappears, abandoning the words.

I marvel at how hard it is to locate the spring the sentences are welling from.

But now the pain, panting, irony, and warmth of the

words are focused on lunatic claims:
Sweet instead of green—that's what the sun likes.
If you eat the atlas, let's whistle the skateboard down the hill.
Tamara drives the sheetmetal dim, and you?
Straighten me in the wrong dental braces, dear sirs, and
you'll get to see a white ermine moth.
In a pale thread the sisters glow.

And then the sentences disappear, too.
Only phrases remain:
In the viola's spray.
The stallion's power, the stallion's power!
Willpower grown gloomy.
A wavering wrench.
A male battle-axe.
A miniature cow.
A fodder-faced self.
Pounding herring in oil.

Then the phrases disappear and are replaced by concepts whose meaning is provided in parentheses:
Cribicus (the luster of bright flowers)
Nuvitation (rhinoplasty for appearance's sake)
Tibalicks (the angle at which a milk can is poured)
Simekabula (the hatred of women in the name of a white
turban)
Jotatus (a headache that can be alleviated with lovage and
blinds)
Vitumation (innocence)
Ellavaclation (the Bible explained through pure reason)

Bullavaclation (the Bible explained through fickle and volatile emotions)

Suddenly words disappear from my dreams altogether.
I miss them, but half a year later, dances are added to these nightly reels of silent film.
The first is a dance of pure sorrow.
I place a Native American headdress on my head. It glows, heavy at first but diminishing, and I can only dance in the circle with the others while it's still burning. Once the feathers have melted, I drape the headdress over my arms like a body.
The headdress smokes, and the eyes whose gaze I live for—they've turned away from me.
The second is a dance of order and the joy of order.
It's an Irish stepdance, and my feet tap the ground regularly, loving the rules. Dust flies.
But I stumble and retreat from the group. I stomp the ground alone, but soon my legs become paralyzed and I wake up dripping in sweat.
I lead the third dance myself.
This dance is airy and dazzling—but don't think this dance is airy.
The room is bright and spacious—but don't think the room is spacious.
This dance is a polonaise—only a fool would believe this dance is a polonaise.
I glide across the room in Hans Christian Andersen's red dancing shoes, cutting diagonally across the room from corner to corner.

I glide alone, and my steps are light; I make arabesques and triple Salchows as I dance.

I glide in spirals, squares, and circles.

I'm fast. I'm Hermes. I'm unattainable.

I'm a liar and the king of thieves.

And when the hands of the first panting person take hold of my tailcoat, I consent to it.

It doesn't matter if my spirals plunge into the depths or take to the sky; at this speed, I'll whirl out of the circle either way.

I stomp my foot on the floor.

My patent leather shoes draw *s*'s and infinity symbols in the air.

The hands of the person dancing behind me pull down on my hips, and the room is filled with the heavy panting of someone else.

I'm so light! In shoes so heavy!

anticipation

Our family has joined Asuntosäästäjät, an organization that builds housing for ordinary people essentially at cost. That means we have such a low profit margin and surplus value that Father has to get another job.

Father goes to work as the film projector repairman at the newly built Helsinki Hall of Culture.

He shows Soviet films in Alppi Auditorium there in the evenings, and Mother and I can go see them for free whenever we like.

We often do want to see the films, but once we know them all by heart, we no longer feel like going and spend the evenings at home instead, just the two of us.

Forty years later she becomes a professor of dramaturgy and goes to work at the very same Hall of Culture.

She visits Alppi Auditorium to view the plays her students have written and directed, and every day she passes the old film projector out on display in the hallway; it looks heavy and pathetic in this age of lightweight electronics.

Father finds it just as hard to get up in the mornings as I do.

We sit on our chairs, irritated and swollen from sleep, while Mother hums and makes coffee.

And Father finds it hard to go to sleep at night, same as me.

It's past eleven at night when he comes home from the Hall of Culture, and he's been on the go since seven in the morning.

Before heading to his job at the Finland–Soviet Union Society, he carries the fruit from the basement up to Mother's store and helps her through the morning rush; then he hurries to work and straight back to the store after work; he stops at home to eat and count the day's earnings and then rushes to the Hall of Culture for the seven o'clock and nine o'clock showings.

But when Father comes home at night, he's too agitated to go to bed, even though he has dark circles under his eyes and his mouth is dry from smoking; instead he pulls out the plans for their two-bedroom apartment in Puotila.

"There's the bathroom."

And night after night Father points his cigarette-stained finger at the bathroom.

"With hot water," Father says.

"Can you imagine?" Mother says.

And Father takes out the tape measure and measures the Asko sofa bed and the dinner table and the shelf over and over; with the help of a ruler he converts yards to inches and fits matches cut to size in the plan.

"The sofa can go there, or?"

"Why not," Mother says.

"And the bookshelf over here, right?"

"That seems like a good spot," Mother says.

Eventually Father gets angry.

"You could at least pretend to be interested!"

"I am, I am," Mother says, flustered, and she comes over to look at the bathroom plans and the matches again.

On Sundays we go on a drive to Puotila in our cream-colored Moskvitch.

The Puotila neighborhood doesn't exist yet, but it will. Father stands among the trees and gestures with his hands: "That's where it's gonna go up, right about there, and I bet that's where the tub goes, with the hot water faucets there; and that's where the other building with the one-bedroom apartments will go, and the shopping center over there, and it'll have whatever you could possibly need: sheets, sausage, restaurants, furniture, perms, saw blades, wallpaper…you name it… No need to go downtown unless you really want to."

On the way back, we feel down, Mother and I: a cow moos in the autumn drizzle, and a hay barn that's been slated for demolition sits hunched in the rain, depressed by the coming progress.

But Father drives the Moskvitch with a sure, determined hand:

"This isn't some hinterland. It'll soon be a city neighborhood where everything is new and serves a purpose."

Mother and I don't care about things serving a purpose. We've come to enjoy our aimless walks along the asphalt streets lined with rundown buildings; the sound of the city's clattering trams and the distant hum of Linnanmäki amusement park; the old linden trees with crooked limbs and the drunkards and their senseless brawling.

But we don't say anything.

Father fixes me with a stern, steely gaze through the rearview mirror:

"And this girl here is going to do better in school. You're applying for secondary school in the spring."

Mother puts up a weak resistance.

Mother has seen so many people forced to continue their schooling, resulting only in tears and disappointment and anemia and poor posture.

But Father refuses to budge.

"She's not dumb, just lazy," Father says.

"She's done fairly well," Mother protests. "That's what her teacher says, too—she's average but sticks to it."

"I'd sure like to see her stick to it for once," Father mutters, speeding up to get the Moskvitch out of the sad, Puotila puddle into which the car has sunk.

I get average grades on my report card, and that spring Father takes me to Kallio Secondary School for the entrance exam.

Kallio Secondary School smells very different from Aleksis Kivi Elementary School.

For four years my elementary school has smelled like rye porridge, fish soup, a dentist's office, and floor wax. But there's no dentist at Kallio Secondary School. Now students can get their teeth cleaned wherever they like. The school doesn't serve any meals either; instead, students either bring their own lunches or choose not eat anything all day, exactly as they please.

I immediately start to like this school, even though the teachers are old and dressed in black and don't smell of lilies-of-the-valley or lipstick or starch; instead they smell of dust and garlic, cigarettes and mothballs.

Everything is large, bright, and spacious at Aleksis Kivi Elementary School.

At Kallio Secondary School the ceiling lights are dim and old-fashioned, and the desks smell of old wood. The stuffed birds are shabby and practically bald, and there's no way they've flown anywhere near a forest in over a hundred years.

The spring sun filters through stained-glass windows on the top landing of the narrow staircase, casting a soft glow over the applicants' heads.

And

she dimly realizes that the school's shabby, old-fashioned appearance, the faint lighting that shies from the new and bright, and the stagnation that smells like moth balls, are all deliberate remnants of culture and civilization.

She watches the teachers coming and going, carrying their binders, books, and maps while wearing heavy, black dresses and suits ill-suited for the spring weather, chalk staining the hems.

She considers whether she might finally be seen in this shabby and sacral environment.

Whether these pale teachers, lost in their own worlds, could in fact want to see her.

And she believes it's possible.

I decide I want to go to secondary school.

I stand in Kallio Secondary School's auditorium holding Father's hand as the principal walks up to the podium in his black suit and begins to read the names of the accepted students.

He says many names, and my name isn't among them.

I open my secret gate in a panic and am already far away in the blue haze when Father suddenly gives my hand a firm squeeze.

"Well then."

"What?" I whisper.

"Congratulations," Father says in a low voice, and I notice he has tears in his eyes.

"What?" I try again, but Father tugs me by the arm out into the sunshine, even as names are still being read.

Outside Father explains that my name was on the list of accepted students, how did I not hear it called out?

"Saisio, Pirkko Helena," Father repeats. "There in the middle. Not a bad way to start."

"Oh," I say weakly, as blood spurts from my nose,

spreading across the front of my green-checked Brigitte-Bardot-style dress.

And

they walk down the hill toward Kallio Market Hall: Father swinging his arms wide as his daughter desperately tries to stop the blood gushing from her nose with a tissue.

They're both far away on this early June afternoon, Father in the future: his daughter has graduated from high school and university and become an economist, then gone on to become the youngest woman ever to receive a doctorate in economics, and she leads the chain of Saisio Imported Goods stores with a firm and assured hand.

And his daughter wanders the world behind her gate, now on alert since the light there has suddenly changed, grown dimmer and richer, as if the stained-glass windows on the top landing of Kallio Secondary School are already refracting the harshest burning rays of the sun.

Father stands in a group of men with his hands in his pockets: calm, stout, serene.

I recognize many of them—unlike Father, they're all still alive.

Hesitantly, I approach Father and touch his arm.

Even through the tweed fabric, I can feel that it's warm.

It's puzzling.

Father glances at me, unsurprised.

"Well then."

"Hey," I say.

"Hey there," Father responds.

I hear the men burst out laughing at someone, not me; and the far-off sound of shattering dishes.

"So you stopped by," I say.

"I did," Father answers.

Father starts turning back toward his friends, and I know I have to hurry.

"So do you know that you've died?" I dare to ask.

"Of course," Father says.

The shattering dishes are now joined by a distant guitar.

Mother is singing "Harbor Nights" somewhere.

"Where have you been?" I ask.

Father gestures broadly with his hand.

"Been flying around as a butterfly mostly," Father says.

"But that's getting boring, too."

I wake up.

It's the morning of Father's funeral.

I miss my mother.

With a career spanning over 40 years, PIRKKO SAISIO is a celebrated author, actress, and director in her native Finland. She has been recognized with many awards, including the 2003 Finlandia Prize, Finland's most prestigious literary prize, for *The Red Book of Farewells*. Her broad literary output includes novels written under the pen names Jukka Larsson and Eva Wein as well as essays, plays, screenplays for TV and film, and even librettos for the ballet. She received her degree in acting from what is now called the Theater Academy in 1975, and she worked there as a professor of dramaturgy between 1997 and 2001. Most recently, she was nominated for the Finlandia Prize for her latest novel *Passio* (Passion, 2021); it is her seventh nomination, more than any other author.

MIA SPANGENBERG translates from Finnish, Swedish, and German into English. Her published translations include works by Finlandia-Prize-winning authors Mari Manninen and Pirkko Saisio and acclaimed children's book author and illustrator Marika Maijala. She was awarded the American–Scandinavian Foundation's 2023 Nadia Christensen Translation Prize for her translation of Pirkko Saisio's *Lowest Common Denominator* (Two Lines Press, 2024). She holds a Ph.D. in Scandinavian studies from the University of Washington, Seattle.